BRIDLEWOOD

(Forgive Me Father, for You Have Sinned)

BRIDLEWOOD

(Forgive Me Father, for You Have Sinned)

C. Frederick Long

SUNSTONE
PRESS

SANTA FE

Sunstone books may be purchased for educational, business, or sales promotional use.
For information please write: Special Markets Department, Sunstone Press,
P.O. Box 2321, Santa Fe, New Mexico 87504-2321.

Book and cover design › R. Ahl
Printed on acid-free paper
∞
eBook 978-1-61139-326-2

ON FILE

WWW.SUNSTONEPRESS.COM
SUNSTONE PRESS / POST OFFICE BOX 2321 / SANTA FE, NM 87504-2321 /USA
(505) 988-4418 / FAX (505) 988-1025

PREFACE

I am a practicing Roman Catholic. Events in my life several years ago led to a devastating revelation. I decided to write this fictional novel as a way to bring closure to a disastrous moment in my life, but it ended up evolving into an intriguing story I am proud to share with the world. It is a fascinating journey into the secret world of a Catholic priest and a married female parishioner, and their journey into the world of carnal sin. The storyline is compelling. It's also reminiscent of a great deal of personal depredation upon my psyche in the not so long ago past.

I could have never attempted this novel were it not for the love and support of my amazing wife, Jayne. She gave me the emotional space to write this story and also endured many long nights of my typing away at my keyboard. She is truly the love of my life and helped me to believe in love again. I can't imagine life without her. My sister, Veronica, was also an integral part in this novel becoming what it is today. Her editing and critiquing skills were the most valuable contributions to the creation of this novel. Her experience as a writer and editor helped give me the tools to transform a *great* story into a *fantastic* story of intrigue and forbidden romance.

Writing this novel was as much a work of inspiration as it was therapeutic. In my opinion, the idea that a Roman Catholic priest must be bound to celibacy for the Church is as ludicrous as it is detrimental to the lives it can destroy as a result. Although there are many heinous acts of immorality that are perpetrated by a few priests, such as child molestation, other casualties are often overlooked as a result of the power they and the Church wield. Corruption, greed, and immorality are present in many aspects of our world, but it shouldn't run rampant throughout the entity charged with the care of our immortal souls.

1
IN THE BEGINNING...

The pivotal moment had arrived to unveil the truth. Curtis Sheffield knew the next few minutes would change the way he viewed life and love for the remainder of his years. He could barely focus on his task through the heavy, all-consuming thoughts thudding around in his head as if on spin-cycle. And they all returned to one question: How did my marriage get so off-track that my wife would fall into the arms of our priest?

Now, as he neared closer to this moment of truth, his mind swam with questions and confusion. *How could my wife of twenty-five, mostly happy years, be having an affair with our priest—the very person charged with our spiritual lives and supposedly ordained by God? Did he seduce her? Did she seduce him?*

A loud, barking dog next to his Jeep startled him, and he was briefly pulled out of his train of thought. It was just someone walking his dog past him down the street, but the distraction still caught him off guard. He scanned the street around him so that he might anticipate any more distractions.

The street where he was sitting was close to downtown, so there was light traffic, but nothing out of the ordinary. There was an abandoned warehouse just across the street from him, where a homeless man sat under the front door awning. He appeared to be sleeping.

As Curtis finished his scan of his surroundings, his thoughts were sucked back into the impending encounter he was about to witness and its possible origins.

Curtis thought, *I've not always been the best husband, and there were those couple of times when I slipped up and betrayed my marriage, but I thought things were improving. We even renewed our vows at our twenty year anniversary. I've read articles about how certain women seek out affairs with their priests, and how there are priests who fall in love with female parishioners.*

It's strange, but as angry as I am, I think I'm also relieved that he chose my wife, and not my son. It's not so much the betrayal of my wife, but combined with the betrayal of my priest, it's almost more than I can bear.

This really fucking sucks. I feel like crying, but I can't. Why can't I cry? Maybe I don't care enough to cry. No, that's not it. Maybe it's just the pure anger and disappointment at the level of betrayal it takes for a wife and a priest to have an affair. This is driving me crazy. God, I wish I could just down all this whiskey in the hopes that it might silence the madness. I could never do this alone. Thank God for Lily and Steamboat. Without them, I'm not sure what I would've done. I didn't think I would feel so much confusion over what's about to happen.

I need to calm down and focus. The betrayal feels like so much more than I can bear, but I need to focus. My redemption is almost certainly at hand.

Janet and Father Richard, your time together in secret is about to run out. I just hope I can keep my cool. God, if you're really there, please give me strength. Hang on Curtis; you can do this.

As Curtis gripped his steering wheel with all his strength, he decided to concentrate on only the adjacent street that would inevitably soon carry Janet's car to its destination. So there he sat, looking at only the empty street, hiding across the way from his wife's office, like some cheap detective novel private investigator. All he needed was a fedora hat and a cigarette to complete the picture.

He'd brought with him a roast beef sandwich that he'd hurriedly thrown together as he left the house. He wasn't even hungry. His knuckles were white from gripping the steering wheel.

He bit his lower lip and felt his knees begin the tremble as another question began to trip him up. *How am I going to react when I see the betrayal for myself?*

Curtis grabbed one of the baby wipes he kept in his Jeep and began to clean the dash and console. It seemed to bring a sense of calm. Then he began running his fingers through his salt and pepper hair and stroking his beard. Then he fiddled with the radio, scanning every station for a familiar song to help calm him down. Then he remembered the flask he had in the middle console. He retrieved it and took a couple of drinks of whiskey. It seemed to help but only for a few moments, because then he saw Janet's car coming down the street toward her office.

As Janet pulled up she just sat there, parked in her car for about five minutes. He could see she was texting on her phone. She finally got out of her new Mercedes, the one she insisted he buy her last Christmas, and she walked into her office. Curtis noticed she was wearing her little black dress with buttons down that back that she only wore when she was going out on the town with her girlfriends, and her long blonde hair was loose and flowing in the wind. She reached up to push a bit of hair out of her face. With a twinge of pain and regret, he realized that lately, her beautiful bright blue-eyes had possessed a new, different gleam. He wondered why he hadn't realized it before now. Curtis took in her slender figure, with her perfect tan, thanks to the tanning bed that Janet had installed in their garage three years ago. Most of the time, she wore business casual dresses and mid heel shoes, but not today. Today, she was wearing stilettos, at least four inches high.

He began to wonder about all of the signs he'd missed as the affair had unfolded right under his nose. What else had he failed to notice as this betrayal was threatening him and his family? He started trying unravel the details of her behavior during the past months, but then, thudding his fists on the steering wheel, he snapped himself out of this particular rabbit hole. There would be time enough to dwell on these things, later.

After about ten minutes, she walked out the back door onto the small wooden porch and began looking around, obviously waiting for him. Thirty seconds later, Father Richard's old green Volvo pulled up. He pulled into the small parking lot and she rushed down the stairs and jumped in his car like she was late for a wedding.

They pulled off with haste and Curtis followed. Curtis wasn't sure where they were going and he wanted to make sure they didn't get out of his sight, so he stayed close enough so as not to lose them but not so close that they would recognize him. His heart raced every time they rounded a corner or made a turn. As they got closer to their eventual destination, Curtis recognized where the rendezvous was going to take place, and his stomach began to toss in his gut.

They headed straight for the rectory, as anticipated. When they arrived, the garage door opened. They pulled inside and closed the door behind them. Curtis pulled his Jeep to the side of the neighborhood street, just around the corner. He quickly worked his way to the side of the rectory between some bushes.

Sweating profusely, and gulping back a jumpy stomach, Curtis neared the kitchen window on the east side of the house. He maneuvered himself between a couple of rose bushes so that he might have a good view inside. His heart was pumping so hard and fast by this time, he imagined they might hear it from within the house. He slowly inched his way against the side of the window and, for a moment, stood silent and motionless.

With one final deep breath to calm himself, he turned his body just enough to peer inside caught his first glimpse of the betrayal.

Janet and Father Richard were drinking wine and laughing. Curtis noticed how Father Richard kept scanning Janet's svelte body, up and down. In between sips, Janet reached out to softly caress his face with the back of her hand. The two acted like teenagers in love. Their constant hungry gaze at one another, their laughing and smiling, combined with the light petting was almost more than Curtis could bear to watch. Yet he continued. Oddly, this overt display was almost therapeutic for Curtis, as if purging him of the anxiety and confusion he'd been battling earlier. It gave him confidence to do what he knew had to be done.

Janet and Father Richard both took a final sip of wine, put their glasses down, and began to embrace one another. Father Richard wrapped his arm around Janet's waist and pulled her in for a long kiss. Janet started unbuttoning his shirt as they started out of the room, just before Curtis lost sight of them. He sat down with his back to the cool bricks of the house, covered his face with his hands, and began to weep.

Curtis's thoughts began to spin out of control again, and he knew he had to regain his composure. He took several deep cleansing breaths and quickly gathered himself, because there was no time for such emotions right now. He had a task to complete and Curtis was intent on seeing it through.

The months leading up to Curtis's witness of the affair were comparably without drama, even while Father Richard and Janet grew to enjoy one another's company more and more. Although neither wanted to acknowledge it, they could see that their friendship was leading to something more. In fact, they might've even feigned resistance through their flirtations until one, seemingly normal, Fall afternoon.

Janet and the rest of the board members were finishing up a meeting in late September. After the meeting, Father Richard asked if Janet would like to go to lunch with him, as they often had many times before. But this time, instead of driving to their favorite restaurant, Father Richard said he felt like cooking lunch at the Parish rectory.

When they got to the house, Father Richard poured Janet and himself a glass of wine and they went into the kitchen where he began to prepare their meal. It was an old family recipe handed down from Father Richard's mother. Spaghetti and meatballs with a homemade marinara sauce that

Father Richard had been cooking since the night before.

With a wink and a chuckle, he said "Janet, this marinara sauce is better than the best sex you'll ever have. My grandmother, a unique and unapologetically straightforward woman, taught me how to make it when I was only thirteen years old. She was my favorite person in the entire world, and loved by all who knew her. She said those same words as she taught me the recipe." He winked again.

They both grinned at one another behind their wine glasses, and took their next sip in unison. Then Father Richard began to plate the meal. He pulled some warm crusty bread from the oven and placed it on the table next to the spaghetti and meatballs and then they prayed over the meal, as they had done at every meal prior.

This time, however, was different. As they ate and drank their wine they began to discuss Father Richard's late wife. He had never really spoken in detail her. Janet and Curtis felt it was a matter best left for Father Richard to mention, so they never broached the subject with him in too much detail.

Father Richard began to talk about her with Janet, and before he could get the first few sentences out of his mouth, he began to cry.

Janet moved from her side of the table and sat in the chair next to him. "Father Richard, it's okay. You can talk to me about it. I'm your friend. You can tell me anything."

He composed himself, and after taking a deep breath, said, "Janet, please just call me Richard. You're not just my friend. You're my best friend."

After that, they both began to cry and shortly thereafter talked about Richard's wife, who had passed away from cancer four years earlier. Richard's pain ran deep at this loss after such a long marriage.

"My wife, Joleen, was more than just a wife and mother. She was my soul-mate and best friend in life. I had no idea how I was going to survive after her death, but the Church gave me comfort and a meaning for my life that seemed to surpass even the great love I had with Joleen. I knew that having a church of my own to watch over and care for was the meaning to my existence. The friendship I've cultivated with you and your family was just the thing I needed to remind me of how special family is to one, and to those who share in its love. *You* have given my life a new meaning, Janet."

This lunch turned into the emotional cleansing that Richard had needed for a long time.

He then said, "Janet, I would like to invite you to accompany me to the prayer room to pray with me. It's a place I always go to be alone with God, but right now, I can't see myself not having you with me."

"I am honored that you've asked me into your sacred space. Of course I'll join you. Thank you, Richard." They then walked down the hallway and downstairs into a large dark room where Richard struggled to find the light switch.

"Too much wine, I think," he said with a chuckle as he turned on the light and smiled.

To the left was a small dark room with a velvet curtain for a door. As he pulled back the curtain and switched on the room's golden lamp, a beautiful altar, of sorts, was revealed, with a large crucifix as its centerpiece.

"I've never felt more in the presence of God as I do at this very moment," Janet said.

They both kneeled before the crucifix and Richard began to pray. As he prayed, Janet reached for Richard's hand. As their hands melted together, it brought chills to Janet's entire body.

When Richard finished with the prayers, he turned to Janet, their hands still clasped together, and said, "I see my late wife in you Janet, and your spirit has touched mine in a way that I had not anticipated. I am powerless to the feelings I have for you right now, in this moment. I feel as though God Himself is laying His hands on us and is speaking to our hearts. God has given you to me and I know you feel it too."

An electric shiver traveled down her spine, and tears sprang forth. "I do," she whispered looking straight into his eyes.

Father Richard looked at the golden glow on Janet's tear-stained face and she appeared like an angel gifted to him by God. He then cradled her face gently in his hands, feeling as if he was receiving a sacrament and also offering up a gift to the Lord in his outstretched palms.

Their eyes remained fixed on one another as he drew her toward him. He hesitated for only a moment to revel in the gift before him. Then he dropped an arm behind her and firmly pulled her in for a long kiss.

They both felt as if the hand of God had reached into their souls and ignited a fire from within them. They slowly began to remove each other's clothing, and Janet said softly, "God has blessed us this day. I will not deny God's will."

Afterwards, they remained for some time holding one another without another word being said until they drifted off to sleep.

Somewhere around 4:30 that afternoon, they woke up feeling a little groggy from the wine, sat up and began to get dressed. Not a word was spoken. When they were dressed, they stood silently looking into one another's eyes, each hoping the other would speak first.

The distant sound of a ticking clock, a neighbor's dog barking, and light neighborhood traffic began to pierce the veil of their sanctum.

Richard finally spoke, "Janet, God has blessed us today, here in this sacred place."

Janet paused for a moment, as reality crept in, threatening the facets of their union. She replied, "I know God is with us, but how do we move forward? This isn't something we can just declare to the world. What would the Church think? What would the congregation think? What would our friends think? Oh God, what will Curtis and my children think?"

She continued, "Richard, I'm in love with you, and I know that you love me, and God has blessed our union here today. But what are we going to do? We have to think about the consequences. We need to work this out in our hearts, alone." She brought a hand up to cover her mouth, as if holding back an avalanche of anxious thoughts.

Richard gently pulled took Janet's hand and held it sandwiched between his. "Janet, please try to relax. There are a lot of questions we will both have to ask ourselves in the upcoming days, and I agree we need to do it alone. God is with us, so let's reflect on that point, and we'll talk it out soon."

After Janet left Richard stood at the front door motionless for a long time.. Then he returned to the prayer room, kneeled in front of the crucifix, and began to silently pray.

Lord, God Almighty, give me the strength to allow this woman into my heart with the depth I have for Your Church. I know You have blessed our union here today, but I ask that You see fit to allow Your Church to bless this union as well. My dedication and gifts to Your Church have served me well in the past, as You well know, but I'm afraid they may not be enough to clear a path for Janet and me. So I ask You, my Lord, if it is Your will for me to leave the Church, then I will do so. Tell me what to do and I will do it. Just make sure to please protect my precious Janet, Your daughter.

He then began to pray the Rosary over and over for almost two hours before he went to his bedroom for the evening. He stopped for a glass of whiskey on his way. As he entered the room, he opened the drawer to his dresser and pulled out his pajamas and changed into them. Walking into the bathroom he gulped the remainder of his whiskey and began to pray the Hail Mary as he brushed his teeth.

As was his habit, he then began to comb just his bushy eyebrows, one meticulous stroke at a time, all the while reciting to his reflection in the mirror, "You are a strong warrior for God and His righteousness belongs to you."

He repeated this phrase over and over and then went back into the bedroom, sat on the floor with his legs crossed, placed his hands together and began to pray The Lord's Prayer. "Our Father, who art in heaven, hallowed be thy name..."

He recited the prayer three times, then got up and walked over to the photograph of his wife on the dresser. He kissed his fingers and placed them on his wife's face and said, "Joleen, I knew you would come back to me, my love. Nothing will stop us from being together. God will see to that. Goodnight my beloved."

The next morning he woke up at five o'clock like he had done every day for as long as he could remember. He went to the bathroom for a piping hot bath. He was averse to showering. He thought civilized people took baths, not showers. He would lie in the bath and wash himself in the same manner every day. He started at his feet and moved up to his head, lathering soap as he went. Once he was sufficiently rinsed, he would pray the Rosary as he pleasured himself, sexually. It gave him clarity of mind to begin the day, but this morning he skipped the masterbation, saying a prayer out loud instead.

He prayed, "Lord, God Almighty, I will, from this day forward, withhold from spilling my seed anywhere but in my soulmate, Janet. Thank you for bringing her to me. I will not forsake You and I will not forsake her, either. Give us strength as we make this worldly journey. Amen."

He then got out of the tub, drained the water and stood in front of the sink. He dried himself, brushed his teeth, ran his hands through what little hair he had, stroked his goatee twice, and again combed his eyebrows.

He repeated, "You are a strong warrior for God and His righteousness belongs to you," over and over again until he was finished combing his eyebrows.

2
IF ANYONE IS ASHAMED OF ME AND MY WORDS IN THIS ADULTEROUS AND SINFUL GENERATION...

As Janet left the rectory, her mind was flooded with confusion. *I've just made love to my priest. I should feel guilty and full of sin, but I don't feel guilty at all. I know God has blessed the union between me and Richard. I can still feel his arms around me and smell his scent on me. He is my salvation and I will embrace him with everything I am. I know he feels the same way, but I hope he can withstand the scrutiny he will have to endure as a result. Please God don't let him change his mind.*

Janet pulled onto her street and noticed that Curtis's car was in their driveway. She looked at her watch and realized at that moment that it was 5:17. Then she reached for her phone, realizing she had forgotten to turn it back on after leaving the board meeting earlier that day. She found twelve missed calls and thirteen unopened text messages.

She had even forgotten to pick the children up from school.

She stopped the car in the middle of the street, trying to think of a plausible reason why she wasn't able to pick up the children, and also why she was unreachable for hours.

She prayed and tried to look normal as she walked toward the front door, desperately trying to gain her composure. She threw open the door with a smile and said, "Hey guys. Sorry I'm late. We had a small crisis at work and I lost track of time. I had to turn my phone off due the sensitivity of the crisis and I literally just got finished dealing with it. Thank you Curtis, for getting the children from school. I'm sorry."

Curtis, cleaning up a few after-school snacks, said, "It's okay, Hon. I understand." But he was wondering why Janet was working so late. She never had before. She always took great pride in being at the school to greet the children. It was usually Curtis who was late coming home. The thoughts were fleeting, but Curtis was beginning to notice that Janet was less and less of a presence when it came to the children lately. He shook off these thoughts when they occurred because Janet had always been a good wife and mother.

Janet went into the bedroom, took off her shoes and then went into the bathroom, locked the door and wept. She began to silently pray for strength and clarity.

Just then, Curtis came into the bedroom and knocked on the bathroom door. "Janet, I have to go to the restaurant and finish prepping for the birthday dinner I'm catering tonight. Are you good with the kids?"

Janet responded, wiping tears from her eyes, "Yes Curtis, go ahead. I'll be out in a minute."

With that, Curtis left the house, got into his Jeep and headed for his restaurant. When he arrived, he walked through the dining room where he was greeted by a few of his loyal customers.

At one of the tables, having dinner as they did several times a week, was Lily, the church secretary, and Cindy, the church's youth director. Lily was a slender woman, in her late fifties. Her hair, black as night and parted in the middle, flowed halfway down her back. She had a "Mona Lisa Smile" that endeared her to many, including Curtis. Cindy was petite and brown-haired. Her smile lit up a room. Although she was in her early fifties, she didn't look a day over thirty-five. They were especially fond of Curtis.

Cindy grabbed Curtis by the hand as he walked past and asked him to join them for a moment.

"Ladies, it would be my pleasure. Give me just a moment and I'll be right back."

He walked over to the bar and asked his manager if everything was going okay for the birthday party they were catering. After learning of a couple of minor snags that had been remedied, Curtis went back to the table where Lily and Cindy were sitting and sat down.

"How are you lovely ladies doing tonight?" Curtis asked with a large, genuine smile.

Cindy responded, "We're doing well, and as usual, enjoying our meal. How are you, Curtis? Lily and I were just discussing Father Richard, and we were wondering if you would weigh in with your opinion, since you and Janet are such good friends with him?"

"Of course I will. I'd be happy to join your conversation." Curtis said as he gestured to the bartender to bring him a drink.

Lily said, "As you know, Curtis, I've been working at the church now, going on ten years. We are just bewildered as to how "social" our priest has become. I know you and Janet are his close friends, but there are a few whispers circulating through the church that Father Richard is, how should I put this, not acting very priestly. Do you know what I mean?"

"I, for one," Cindy interjected, "think it's a great thing. Father Richard is engaging the community and making friends in a way that no priest I've ever known has done. I think it's a breath of fresh air."

"Well I don't agree." Lily responded. "A priest should be more reserved and conservative with his parishioners, if you will, and much more conservative. I like that he's active in the community, and I know he's your close friend, Curtis, and I don't mean to offend, but I think he socializes too much."

Curtis took a sip of his whiskey and replied, "I actually agree with both of you, in a way. Yes, Father Richard is my friend, but he's befriended Janet much more. He is very active with Janet's charity and he does tend to socialize more than the average priest, but I also believe it's a breath of fresh air to have him so engaged in activities that are not normally associated with being a priest. And it's nice to have someone who has brought some added happiness to Janet's life. As you both know, I'm very busy with the restaurant and the catering business. It's nice to know that someone like Father Richard is in Janet's and the kid's lives like he is." Curtis chuckled a bit, and added, "If he weren't my priest, I'd have a mind to be jealous of all the time he spends with my wife, but as it is, it does bring me peace of mind knowing he's so accessible to my family."

Lily nodded her head in agreement and said, "I can see where your coming from, Curtis, but from the perspective of others, but it does seem as if he is acting in a way that is unbecoming as a priest."

Cindy interrupted with a laugh, playfully tapping Lily on the hand, "Lily, you're just being a prude. Not all of us Catholics are as old-fashioned thinking as you. I like him."

Lily laughed, "You're probably right, Cindy. It's just harder for some of us to accept change in the behavior of our priests. When you grow up in a strict Catholic household, like I did, it's just hard to loosen up. But I'm trying, and maybe after a few more beers, I'll change my mind."

"Well," Cindy said, "as a counselor at the youth center, as well as our youth director, I can tell you that the kids who have come into contact with Father Richard are highly impressed with him. We often have him and Janet coming in to help with some of the more troubled youth and they've both made a positive impact in their lives. Father Richard seems to have a better understanding of how to deal with those kids than our other priests ever did. Maybe the fact that he was married and had children of his own has given him a better understanding of the real world that other priests often have a hard time relating to."

"I agree," Curtis responded. "He's been more impactful in our community than our other priests have been, and Janet has often told me about how wonderful he is, with his involvement in the community."

"I do agree with you as well." Lily said. "But I just think it's going to bite him in the ass if he's not careful."

"You really are such a cynic, Lily," Cindy responded, laughing, "All those years in the FBI have left you with no hope in humanity, hasn't it?"

"Maybe it has, Cindy." Lily shrugged."

Curtis laughed, "I've seen him after several whiskeys. Let's just say, his Italian roots come out after he's had a few, and it's reminiscent of a Godfather/Goodfellas movie. He's quite a character when he lets his guard down a little."

Cindy laughed, "Now, *that* I would love to see."

Curtis chuckled, put his glass on the table, and rose, saying, "Ladies, I'm going to have to leave this conversation here for now. I have to get back to the kitchen and help finish the prep for the party later tonight." He smiled warmly at each of them. "Thank you for your business, as usual. I'm sure we can pick up with this conversation again real soon. Take care."

Lily and Cindy each stood up and hugged Curtis, bidding him a good night. As Curtis walked toward the kitchen, he felt a hand on his shoulder. Cindy said to him, "Curtis, it's been far too long since I've seen you for a haircut. You're not cheating on me with another hair stylist are you?" she said with a wink and a smile.

"No Cindy,' Curtis responded, "I just thought with your new duties as the church's youth director, you would not have much time for your hair business. I was out of town a couple of weeks ago and I stopped at a barber shop and got it cut. It wasn't as good as you, but it got the job done."

"Well," Cindy exclaimed, "You are due for a proper haircut. I have moved my salon into my house since taking the job as youth director. It is going to save me money over having to pay for my space at the salon, and I can still take care of my favorite and loyal customers. You call me tomorrow and I'll schedule you for later this week. How's that sound?"

"Sounds great to me, Cindy," Curtis said. "I'll call you tomorrow."

Cindy smiled and reached out and gave Curtis a pat on the back as she smiled and walked away.

3
GOD BLESSED THEM AND SAID TO THEM...

Father Richard had been leading their parish for the past year and a half. He was a five foot six, two hundred pound man of Italian descent who hailed from New York City. Although Father Richard was an older man at sixty-three years old, with thinning, almost-balding hair, he had quite a robust goatee. His goatee, with its splotches of white, appeared haphazardly groomed. He was always wearing his black clergy shirt and white collar with black pants and black shoes.

While having dinner at Curtis and Janet's home shortly after his arrival to the Church, Father Richard had shared how his appointment to the priesthood had come about.

He had been a Deacon at his Catholic church in New York, where he lived a very content life with his wife, Joleen and two children. After thirty years of marriage, he learned his wife had contracted stage four liver cancer that had moved to her brain. After two very intense years of cancer treatment and several surgeries, his wife finally succumbed to the cancer.

He was so devastated to lose his wife that he almost turned away from God and the Church. Fortunately for him, an older priest in his Parish personally shepherded him and, after many months of council, Deacon Richard decided that God was calling him to the priesthood.

The death of his wife had become the catalyst which propelled him head first into the Church's patriarchy. However, there was just one obstacle that he had to overcome before he could officially become a priest. Pope Francis had to give him special dispensation to become a priest, because the Catholic Church tends to frown on formerly married men becoming priests. But since Deacon Richard had led a seemingly impeccable life and his wife had passed away, the Pope saw fit to allow him to become a priest in the Roman Catholic Church.

Two years and three churches later, Father Richard noticed there was an opening for a new priest at a small Catholic Church in Bridlewood, North Carolina. His wife and he had spent a long weekend there in the late seventies and they both fell in love with the beautiful countryside, the atmosphere, and the mountains that go on for miles and miles. They loved it so much that they would vacation there at least once a year, and oftentimes, twice.

So when he noticed the opening, he jumped at the chance to be transferred there. After some deliberation, he found himself the sole priest of Our Lady of Damascus Catholic Church, in which he found the welcoming hospitality of the community, and the friendship of Curtis and Janet.

Curtis and Father Richard both enjoyed relaxing with a nice cigar and a good Irish whiskey. They would often gather with other parishioners at Curtis and Janet's house to have dinner, play poker and enjoy the fellowship. Sunday Mass even seemed a little more enjoyable now that Curtis and Janet had developed such a special bond with their spiritual leader and friend. Janet also invited Father Richard to join the Board of Trustees of her local charity for the homeless.

There were many in the Parish however, that took a dim view of having a priest that had been previously married. Many Catholics, especially those who were older and lived a more conservative faith, thought a priest should never know the emotional and spiritual bond that a married couple share. It would preclude him from being an objective advocate for God. How could he be an effective priest? After all, being married to the Church, as a priest is so bound, is a marriage that cannot be forsaken or clouded by the knowledge of such a union as between a man and a woman.

Others however, believed a priest that has been previously married is the perfect vessel for which God could counsel such a family oriented religion. Therefore why not allow a man who is widowed the chance to shape the spiritual well being of a Parish? Who better to counsel such a Parish, than one who has known the meaning of what it is to be married? In theory, it makes logical sense.

But nonetheless, the Catholic Church is in fact, beginning to split down the middle about this subject and everyone is choosing a side. But for this small Catholic church in rural Appalachia, it was to become the catalyst for the biggest scandal this town had ever seen.

As tensions about Father Richard's previous marriage made its way throughout the Parish, a thriving friendship was growing between Father

Richard, Curtis and Janet. Curtis and Janet's children were also reaping the benefits of that friendship.

The church also had a school, beloved and supported by all in the church community. Curtis and Janet's three children all attended Our Lady of Damascus Catholic school. It was a humble and satisfying feeling for this family to have the ear of their priest, especially a priest, who, after only a year and a half, was now considered part of the family. He had dinner at least once a week with Curtis and Janet's family. And now that he was on the board of Janet's charity, it seemed as though there was no stopping this trio of friends.

As the months went by, Janet and Father Richard began spending more and more time together. They would often have lunch, while discussing projects for Janet's charity and organizing church events. Janet was excited for her priest to be involved with her charity. Having a Catholic priest actively involved in any charity is a huge plus. After all, the Catholic Church is known for its unstoppable influence among charitable organizations. Having Father Richard as an advocate for Janet's charity was paramount to its continued success. Janet and Father Richard were becoming quite the power couple when it came to the recognition that the charity was beginning to get. Janet and Father Richard hosted many fundraisers, and the donations were pouring in.

At Sunday Mass, Father Richard and Janet were often teased about their friendship, and how they made a better couple than Janet and Curtis. This was obviously said in jest, and in the presence of Curtis and Father Richard. In hindsight however, it should have been easy to see that the friendship Janet and Father Richard had cultivated was becoming more and more intimate, and more dangerous.

As the days passed after Father Richard and Janet's first sexual encounter, and the next Sunday grew closer, Janet began to feel more and more anxious about Sunday Mass. She and Richard hadn't spoken since the encounter. She couldn't get it off her mind. Was it a mistake? Was it fate? Was it God's will and divine intervention? Was it true love? She was beginning to second guess herself, and these were the questions that burned into Janet's psyche every moment of every day since the encounter. She dared not reach out to Richard for fear of what he might say to her. She was growing apprehensive at the idea of seeing him face-to-face. Sunday morning was here, and still not a word from Richard.

Janet and Curtis got themselves and the children ready for Mass as they had every Sunday morning for the last twenty-five years. While they were eating breakfast, one of the children asked what time Father Richard was coming for dinner this evening?

Janet's mind went numb with fear and anxiety. She didn't know what to say. She turned to Curtis and said, "What time do you think, honey?"

He looked at her with a slightly puzzled look and responded, "He usually shows up here around four pm. Is there a reason why that would be different today?"

"Of course not," Janet said with a slightly trembling voice.

"Are you feeling okay?" asked Curtis. "You seem a little off this morning."

Janet cleared her throat with a slight cough and replied, "I think I'm just tired. It's been a tough week at the foundation. I'll be okay."

With that, they gathered themselves and left for Sunday Mass.

When they arrived at the church they were greeted, as usual, at the front door by Father Richard. He was in good spirits and shaking hands and smiling with everyone as they walked into the church. As usual, Father Richard welcomed Janet and Curtis with a warm smile and a loving hug for them all.

As he hugged Janet, he whispered into her ear, "Please come to my office after Mass. We should speak."

She just smiled and said, "It's good to see you Father. We're looking forward to dinner with you tonight at our house." It was all she could do to keep from collapsing under the pressure she was feeling. She could feel her knees weakening and her palms moistening with sweat as she dug her nails into them. As she walked past him into the church she wiped her right hand on her dress to wipe away the sweat, reached out and grabbed Curtis's hand, looked at him, and managed to show a smile. For the moment, the anxiety seemed to wane, just a little.

As they all took their seats in the pew, Janet kneeled and began to pray, as she always did prior to Mass. Before she knew it, Mass was beginning. The mood was much the same as it always had been in church and Janet participated in the Mass much more relaxed than she thought she would. Never mind the thoughts of her infidelity that kept racing through her mind. Those thoughts however, seemed subdued, almost non existent, and were snuffed out immediately. She hadn't anticipated the peace that came over her during Mass.

When Father Richard had finished with the reading of the Gospel and was beginning his Homily, he paused for about ninety seconds. Nothing was said. The church was eerily silent. The parishioners began to look at each other with confusion and shuffle in their seats.

As it was beginning to feel beyond awkward, and few rumblings emerged from the pews, Father Richard, yelled, with a voice that thundered through the church, "Amen. Amen indeed! It's time we repent for our sins."

Curtis leaned over and whispered into Janet's ear with a hint of laughter in his voice, "Must be some Southern Baptist in his lineage."

Janet did not respond. She just stared at Father Richard with a look of bewilderment. If it weren't for her makeup, she thought, everyone would notice how pale she'd suddenly become.

What is he about to say? she wondered, as she felt her legs beginning to shake.

"Are you okay?" Curtis whispered.

Janet just nodded as she placed her hand on Curtis's knee, clenching it tightly.

Then Father Richard stepped down off the altar and began to walk amongst the congregation. He began randomly tapping parishioners on the tops of their heads, calling out loud as he tapped, proclaiming, "You're a sinner, you're a sinner, you're a sinner." He came to Curtis and Janet's pew and placed his hand on Janet's head and said, with a comedic lilt in his voice, "And you, Janet, are most definitely a sinner of grand magnitude."

He laughed, and the entire congregation laughed along with him.

Janet was able to crack a sheepish grin of amusement, while she clenched her teeth.

Father Richard followed the laughter with a statement that explained how he was using theatrics to illustrate a point. He thanked everyone for indulging him and he returned to the lector's podium to begin his Homily.

At that moment, Janet could feel her body completely fall back into the pew, much more relaxed. She let go of Curtis's leg, not realizing her knuckles were white from the intense pressure she'd inadvertently had on his knee. She looked at Curtis and said, "Wow, that was something, wasn't it?"

Curtis chuckled.

After Mass, everyone gathered in the great hall to socialize and greet one another as was always the tradition. While everyone mingled and the kids played outside, Father Richard approached Curtis and Janet and asked if he could borrow Janet for a few minutes. He had some things he wanted to discuss with her concerning the homeless charity. They excused themselves and left for Father Richards's office.

As they entered the office, Father Richard closed the door behind them and asked Janet to join him on the couch.

Janet was silent, waiting for Richard to speak first.

He looked into her eyes and said with the softest voice he could muster, "Janet, I am truly..." Before he could continue, there was a knock at the office door. He got up from the couch and went to the door, opening it with a hint of anger at the disruption.

"What is it Lily?" he asked his church secretary.

Lily responded, "We need you for just a moment Father. There's a family downstairs that needs a blessing as they leave today. It's important. Their son is sick and is having an operation this week. It will only take a moment. I apologize for the interruption, Janet."

Janet nodded her head and said, "Please go, Richard. I'll wait here. It's okay."

As Janet sat in the silence, she contemplated the words Richard had spoken. "Janet, I am truly..."

I am truly what? Janet thought. *Truly sorry? Truly tempted by you, but...*

Truly, truly, truly. That's all she could think of. Nothing else went through her mind for the twenty minutes she sat there, alone in his office.

Finally, Richard came back into the office, closed the door behind him, and sat down on the couch beside Janet. He grabbed Janet's hand, realizing that they were clammy and cold. "Are you feeling okay Janet?" he asked.

She responded, "Please Richard, just say what it is you want to say. Please."

He looked into her eyes once again and said, "Janet, I am truly and deeply, with all I am, in love with you. I spent all week in deep prayer and meditation with our Lord, and He has spoken to me in words clearer than any I've heard before. He has given His blessing to us. But for obvious reasons, we will need to proceed with great caution. God may bless our union, but the world will have a different view of our relationship. So, until we figure out a plan, we must be careful and discreet. Only God sees our great love for one another, and He alone will see us through this process. We must listen only to Him and let Him guide us."

Janet was silent. She looked into Richard's eyes and, after a brief pause, she smiled as a tear rolled down her cheek.

Richard reached out to wipe away her tear with his thumb, placed his fingers behind her head, and pulled her to him. Their lips met, softly. With that, Richard stood up, took Janet's hand and lifted her off the couch.

He opened the door, and as she walked away, Richard said, "I'll see you guys at four for dinner. I can't wait."

When Janet got downstairs Curtis and her children were waotomg. Most everyone else had already left.

As they were walking toward the exit, Lily stopped Jan, grabbing her by the hand, and with a hint of sarcasm, said, "I just want to thank you, Janet, for being such a good friend to Father Richard. There are those in this parish who are still unsure of having a priest who was formerly married. They're afraid his knowledge of being married will tempt him to want to be unfaithful to the Church and betray his vows of celibacy. It brings all of us great joy to see how your family has taken him in and made him feel so welcome in our community. Please accept our gratitude."

Janet smiled in bewilderment and nodded. After all this time, to have Lily acknowledge her in such a way was puzzling. Lily was not the most sociable type. In her ten years as the church secretary and priest's assistant, she hadn't made very many friends, with the exception of Cindy, the church's youth director.

As Janet and her family drove away, all Janet could think about was Richard, and their declaration of love for one another.

The only thought going through Janet's mind right now was, *Oh my God, I'm in love with my priest.*

When Janet and Curtis got home and the children began to play, Curtis asked Janet again, "Are you sure you're okay? You've been acting a little strange today, and during Mass I thought you were going to cut off the circulation to my leg when you grabbed my knee so hard."

Janet laughed and said, "I was just shocked and amazed at the stunt Father Richard pulled during the Homily. It surprised me when he tapped me on the head and called me a big sinner. That's all."

Curtis nodded and smiled, went to the fridge to get a beer, and then went into the living room to watch football.

Janet began to prepare for the dinner they were having with Father Richard and a few of their friends later that afternoon. Sally and Bob from across the street were coming. Sally, a slender redhead, was a stay-at-home mom for their two children. She was very opinionated and not afraid to verbally spar with anyone. Bob, a well respected divorce attorney, was a burly man with a full beard. He loved his red wine and could drink two bottles with ease—three if they were from France. He'd never met a red wine from France that he didn't love, and he thought the French made the best wine in the world. They usually went to the Saturday evening Mass because Bob was an avid golfer and never missed an early Sunday morning tee time. Sally and Janet were very close and every so often, Sally would help out with Janet's charity.

Then there was Chris and Amy. They, and their five children had all been members of Our Lady of Damascus since birth. Amy and Janet grew up on the same street as one another and they bonded instantly as toddlers. They were best friends. In fact they were more like sisters than friends. Not a day went by that Janet and Amy wouldn't talk on the phone or have lunch together. Amy, a slightly pudgy brunette, was the director of the local Chamber of Commerce. And she loved her art. She would often speak about her favorite artists for hours on end.

Her obstetrician husband, Chris, was often absent from these get-togethers because it seemed he was always on call and delivering babies. He was a tall man of about six feet four inches who had played basketball for Kentucky. Although an attractive man, he was completely bald, and that was often a source of tension for him. He'd tried varying hair pieces over the years, but finally, two years ago, he succumbed to the fact that 'bald is beautiful,' and gave up the quest for the full head of hair he's once sported as a handsome college basketball player who was never without a beautiful woman on his arm. But Amy stole his heart during his senior year and they never looked back. She supported him through medical school, and he graduated at the top of his class.

Curtis met Chris at the door with a glass of whiskey as he and Amy walked in around four. Chris and Curtis had become very good friends as well. Chris delivered all three of Curtis and Janet's children. It was a running joke between the two of them that Chris had seen Janet's vagina more than Curtis ever had. They played poker together, and when Chris was available, they would play golf together with Bob and Father Richard. For an older man, Father Richard was a really good golfer.

Father Richard arrived about fifteen minutes later and Curtis greeted him with a hug and an offer for him to have a drink.

Father Richard said, "How about an Irish whiskey, neat?"

"Big surprise," Curtis said, and quickly served up Father Richard his favorite twenty year old Irish whiskey, which they kept prominently displayed atop Curtis's home bar.

Father Richard took his drink and excused himself into the kitchen to see if Janet needed any help, and Curtis returned to the living room.

Father Richard made his way to the kitchen. "Can I help?" he asked as he walked up behind Janet, putting his hand on her shoulder.

"Of course you can, Richard," she said. She turned around and placed her hand just under his scrotum and gave it a slight massaging with a rather happy smile on her face.

At that moment Janet heard footsteps coming from down the hall so she pulled away from Richard and said, "Father Richard, why don't you start by peeling the potatoes."

Richard reached for the potatoes and started peeling as Janet's daughter, Cassandra entered and asked if she could help. Cassandra was ten years old and loved helping her mom and dad in the kitchen.

Janet picked her up and placed her on the counter with a bowl of salad and a mixing spoon.

"Thanks mommy." Janet kissed her on the forehead and they continued preparing the meal. Father Richard looked at Janet, raised his eyebrows and gave her a slight grin. Janet smiled, but immediately turned her attention to helping her daughter. Richard's grinned quickly vanished into a slight frown, perhaps a slight twinge of jealousy.

Father Richard looked at Cassandra and said, "Cassie, how are you today?"

"My name is Cassandra, Father. Please call me Cassandra. I hate the name Cassie."

"Father Richard, Cassandra no longer wants to be called Cassie, so we are respecting her decision. Cassandra, I apologize, but I forgot to tell Father Richard."

Father Richard looked back at Cassandra and said, "I apologize Cassandra. I did not realize. Please forgive me."

Cassandra ignored Father Richard and continued mixing the salad. Father Richard looked at Janet and Janet mouthed the words, "I'm sorry" and they continued to prepare the meal. Father Richard turned toward the counter and lowered his head, upset that he could not make a much wanted connection with Janet's daughter.

A few minutes went by before Janet heard a knock at the door. "That must be Lily" Father Richard said.

"Lily? What is she doing here?" Janet asked.

Father Richard said she had asked him if she could join them for dinner, and since she'd never asked for such a thing for as long as Father Richard had known her, he felt obliged to invite her.

Janet smiled and appeared gracious about her surprise attendee, but in her mind she was contemplating the words that Lily had spoken to her as she left the church earlier that day. Janet was becoming paranoid that Lily somehow knew something was going on between her and Richard. Janet wasn't sure what Lily was up to, but coming to dinner for socialization was definitely not why she was there. Janet knew that she was going to have to do something about Lily. She didn't know what needed to be done, but Lily was definitely going to be a problem.

As everyone arrived, the house began to fill with laughter and conversation.

Amy joined Janet and Father Richard in the kitchen as they went to check on the potatoes.

Amy said, "Father Richard, why have you decided that we should abstain from meat on Fridays? That practice went out in the seventies. You're supposed to be a progressive priest. After all, you were married for Christ's sake. Why be so strict?"

Father Richard opened his mouth to answer when Janet interjected, "Amy, you know Father Richard is old school when it comes to some of the practices of the Catholic Church. He and I have spoken for hours about his love of the old Church, prior to the sixties. I for one, find it refreshing. I love it. Tell her Father Richard. Don't let Amy bully you." Janet lightly punched him in the arm and they laughed.

"Well," Father Richard said with a wink, "It looks like she's said it for me. But she's right. I do prefer the older ways." He lifted his glass for one last swallow, and said, "At that, ladies, I need to go refill my whiskey glass. Please excuse me." Father Richard kissed each on their cheeks and left for the kitchen.

Amy, touching her cheek lovingly, said, "Well I will say this for him, Janet. He does have a sophisticated charm that's very becoming."

Janet peeked around the corner to glance at him, then turned to Amy, saying, "He does have a sexy, older man appeal." They both smiled.

Curtis, Chris and Bob were all sitting in the living room watching football on the big-screen TV when Father Richard walked into the room.

Curtis said, "It's about time you come hang out with the men. You spend entirely too much time with my wife, Father Richard. If you weren't my priest, I'd swear you two were having an affair." They all laughed as Father Richard sat in the chair next to Curtis.

Father Richard laughed again and said, "Curtis, if I weren't a priest, you would be right my brother." He slapped Curtis on the arm as Curtis chuckled.

"Father Richard," Curtis exclaimed, "You are the best priest I have ever known. Your sense of humor ain't that bad, for a Northerner, and you're the only man I've played golf with that has beaten Chris. It's a nice change of pace from Chris constantly winning all the cash every time we play."

Amy, Sally, Lily and Janet were all in the kitchen getting the meal together. It was inevitable, every time this group got together, that the men ended up in the living room watching some sports on television, and the women ended up in the kitchen preparing the meal. The only change was during the spring and summer months, when the men gathered on the back deck, cooking on the grill. Curtis even had a television mounted on the wall of the back deck, just for watching sports out there.

As the women were finishing up the meal prep, Janet said, "It's so refreshing to have Father Richard as part of our Sunday dinners. Don't you girls agree?"

Sally laughed, "Janet, you just say that because you have a secret crush on him." They all laughed, but Janet was secretly thinking, *It's more than a crush. I'm madly, deeply in love with the man.*

Janet said, "You girls are crazy. He is charming and very handsome, for an older man, but he's my priest, for God's sake."

"We know, Janet." Amy winked at her. "We're just teasing you. You guys just spend so much time together at the church and at your work. You spend more time with him than you do your own husband. It's just funny is all."

"I know." Janet said. "But he's been so helpful with my charity. I realize the homeless community is not exactly like Raleigh's, but it's significant enough, and Father Richard has helped to double the amount of money we have been able to raise in the last year, alone. We have three shelters, as you know, Sally. They're all thriving with funds that allow us to keep the doors open, and we've made great strides in getting a lot of them jobs and housing. Father Richard is just so amazing, and talented, and compassionate. He embodies the qualities that, I believe, belonged to Jesus. My heart is so full when I am in his presence. I never could have imagined a better man to be our priest at Our Lady of Damascus. We are truly blessed to have him in our lives. I hope he never leaves."

Sally and Amy both took a sip of their wine and peeked at each other over their wine glasses, grinning and raising their eyebrows at Janet's infatuation. The odd part of this entire conversation was the fact that Lily never said a word the entire time. She just stood there smiling and nodding her head as each woman spoke.

They served dinner about ten minutes later and, as everyone gathered around the dinner table, Father Richard began tapping his glass. He said, "I would like to thank our gracious host, Janet, for this wonderful dinner, and I would also like to say thank you to Lily, for accepting our invitation to join us here this evening. Thank you for coming, Lily. We love you. With that being said, let us pray. "Bless us O Lord, and these Thy gifts, which we are about to receive from Thy bounty. through Christ, our Lord. Amen." Father Richard sat down and they all began to eat.

As they began the meal, Janet looked across the table into Richard's eyes, and as he looked back at her, and they both smiled at one another, he gave her a wink. Then Janet's attention turned to Lily.

Lily was staring at her and Father Richard with piercing scrutiny.

A chill ran down Janet's back. Janet thought to herself, *Something definitely has to be done about Lily.*

4
FOR THE WAGES OF SIN...

After dinner, everyone chipped in to help clean up, except Lily. Lily excused herself, saying she had some things to do at home. Janet and Father Richard walked her to the door and, as Lily stepped off the front porch, she turned and said, "It really is inspiring to see how well the two of you have shown that priests are just like the rest of us lay people and desire companionship and the secular ways of the world, and yet still maintain the integrity of Catholicism. Thank you so much for the lovely dinner, Janet. I'm sure I'll see you at the church this coming week. Father, it was a pleasure. Goodnight."

Then she turned, walked to her, 1972 Chevy truck, and drove away.

As they stood on the porch, trying desperately to understand what Lily meant, Janet and Father Richard just looked at each other, and then simultaneously asked, "What was that?"

Janet then said, "Lily knows something is going on between us. We are going to have to do something about her."

Richard took a deep cleansing breath and stroked his goatee. After a moment, he finally said, "Don't worry about Lily. I'll speak with her on Tuesday and find out what she knows, if anything. Don't worry Janet. I'll take care of it. I promise."

Janet sighed in relief, "Okay Richard, I'll leave it to you for now."

With that, they both agreed they needed to join the group and pretend not to be in love as they socialized for the rest of the evening.

Janet's children and their friends had already gone outside to play because they weren't allowed to play video games when company was over. The adults had gathered downstairs in the rec room to watch football and just generally socialize.

The guests usually found themselves gathering around the bar Curtis had built out of wormy-maple. Curtis was proud of that bar. He often spoke of how it took him six months to build it just the way he wanted it. At the end of the bar was a humidor where Curtis and Father Richard kept their favorite cigars they liked to enjoy on the patio just outside the rec room, though the two had not shared a cigar in some time.

Curtis spoke up, "Gentlemen, would you like to join me on the patio for a cigar?

Bob, Chris and Father Richard all gathered with Curtis at the humidor and each picked out a cigar. Curtis poured each a whiskey and they headed outside.

The centerpiece of the patio was a large, round, marble table that had belonged to Curtis's grandfather. His grandfather handcrafted it out of a single slab of marble. It weighed several hundred pounds, but was an extraordinary honey beige with beautifully orchestrated lines running through every square inch. Six hand crafted wooden, high-back chairs surrounded it. Curtis had the ash wood chairs designed and built specifically to compliment the marble table. In the center of the table was a round, eighteen-inch, lead crystal Wedgewood ashtray with slots for six cigars.

They all settled into chairs around the table, and began to light their cigars. The sweet smell of the tobacco quickly filled the night air and hung over the men like a slowly wafting cloud. The overhead light from the roof of the patio's overhang danced through the cloud of smoke, reminiscent of the Northern Lights. It brought a sense of calm over each of the men, and not a word was spoken between them for at least five minutes as they enjoyed the experience of each slow draw from their cigars along with the inevitable sip of whiskey that followed.

Father Richard broke the silence, "Gentlemen, I can surely say that every time I enjoy a cigar and whiskey in the fellowship of friends, as we are here tonight, it's a close to Heaven as any man can see here on Earth. Savor the moment, for in these times, moments such as this are few and scarce. God is good. Is He not?"

All four men raised their glasses and clinked them together above the crystal ashtray as Curtis said, "Amen brothers, amen." And they all took a sip of whiskey.

Not two seconds later, Janet opened the door, stuck her head out and said, with a wink directed at Father Richard, "Gentlemen, would you kindly come back inside? We women are feeling a bit neglected."

Father Richard stood up, "You're absolutely correct, Janet. Gentlemen, let's ignore our beautiful hostess and her friends not one moment longer."

With that, they all headed back inside. As Curtis glanced back at the table and chairs, taking note of the cloud of cigar smoke as it dissipated and drifted away.

Everyone continued to enjoy themselves as the evening wore on. But eventually, the group got smaller as Chris and Amy left for home, and then Sally and Bob.

Around ten all who remained were Janet, Curtis and Father Richard. Curtis saw that Janet and Father Richard were deep into a discussion about the church and the charity, so he excused himself to get the children ready and tucked into bed. Curtis told Father Richard goodnight and gave Janet a kiss.

As Curtis went upstairs and down the long hallway into the bedroom, Richard turned to Janet and said with a twinge of jealousy, "I never realized how much it bothers me to see him kiss you."

Janet whispered, "Me too. It makes me sick to think of anyone's lips on mine except yours. I wish we could be together as husband and wife, Richard. I'm ready to be yours alone and I know God wants the same for us. We have to find a way to make it happen."

"Remember," as Richard brushed his hand against hers, "it is God's will for us to be together. Trust in Him that he will make it happen, on His timeclock, not ours. I want us to be together as well, but God has a plan and we would do well to abide by it. In the meantime, I would appreciate it if you could try to refrain from being intimate, both physically and emotionally, with Curtis. You are mine and I am yours in God's eyes. I know it will be difficult, but we must try our best to maintain the integrity of our union, despite the obstacles that are in our path. It is God's way of testing the strength of our love for one another as we wait for the day we can be together in the sight of everyone."

Janet began to cry. "You are so right, Richard. And you are so wise and wonderful. No wonder God has chosen you to be His priest for our church. I love you more and more as each hour passes. And I agree, so I will refrain from being intimate in any way with Curtis. I can do it, and he'll never suspect a thing. I *am* yours Richard, and I always will be."

They then walked to the front door and Janet turned off the front porch light. They stepped out onto the porch and Janet shut the door behind them. They looked around to make sure no one was watching, then embraced for a sensual goodnight kiss. Richard's hand gently caressed her lower back. They held hands until their outstretched arms could no longer allow their hands to touch as he walked away.

Janet watched as his Volvo drove out of sight.

As she turned to go inside, she noticed a distant pair of headlights suddenly turn on. She squinted to see what it was, but all she could make out in the dark was the faint outline of an old pickup truck. It made a whining noise as it turned away.

She thought to herself, *Could that have been, Lily?*

She quickly dismissed the thought, for all she could think about was Richard and how much she loved him. Janet then walked back into the house and into their bedroom to find Curtis fast asleep. She put on her nightgown, brushed her teeth, said a prayer, and got in bed, dreaming of what it would be like to be the wife of a priest. She thought, *How magnificent it would be and how pleased will God be that I am married to one of His shepherds as he tends His flock.* With that thought, Janet smiled and dozed off.

The next morning Janet was making breakfast when she received a text message from Lily. Lily wanted to meet for lunch. Before responding, Janet sent a text to Richard to tell him about the mysterious invitation.

Richard called immediately.

She'd barely said hello when Richard interrupted her and said, as if out of breath, "Do not meet with Lily until you and I have a chance to talk."

"Why do you sound as if you are out of breath, Richard?"

"I'm just finishing my morning routine, but it's important you understand something. Last night when I left your house, I was followed by Lily. As I rounded a corner heading out of your neighborhood, I noticed her truck behind me. I caught a glimpse of it under a street lamp in my side view mirror. I think you may be right Janet. She's suspicious of us."

"I told you so." Janet rubbed her forehead. "I have a meeting at ten this morning. I'll tell Lily I can't meet with her until tomorrow. I'll meet you at the rectory after the meeting, and we can discuss our strategy for dealing with this problem. I love you. Talk to you soon."

With that, Janet hung up and went to call the children and Curtis to the dining room for breakfast.

When breakfast was over, Curtis kissed Janet goodbye and left to drop the children at school on his way to work. Janet kissed the children and told them to have a great day, and that she would see them after school. Then she quickly cleaned up the breakfast dishes.

Once finished, Janet texted Lily: *Good morning Lily. Thank you for your invitation to lunch. I would love to, but I have meetings all day. Would tomorrow at noon be okay?*

Lily quickly responded: *Yes. That will be fine.*

Sighing in relief, Janet gathered her keys, her purse, and her leather satchel, and left for work.

When she arrived at her office, she unlocked and opened the front door as usual. But when she glanced down at the floor just inside the door, she found a sealed white envelope with only her name on it. She picked up the envelope and went to her office. Once settled at her desk, she picked up the envelope and opened it. Inside was a single sheet of paper with only a few words typed in bold capital letters. It simply stated, "**FATHER RICHARD IS A PRIEST. HAVE YOU NO SHAME?**"

Janet's heart skipped a beat and she felt the color drain from her face. This had to be from Lily. What was happening? Janet felt faint.

She got up slowly from her desk, feeling a little wobbly and shaken. She made her way to the office kitchen and made herself a cup of coffee, and they sat down. Just as she was processing everything that had happened in the past week, her employees began trickling in and making small talk with her. She had to focus on her work and try her best to put the events of the morning out of her mind just long enough to get through her meeting and get to Richard.

It seemed like every minute was passing slower and slower. Like her body were moving in slow motion, yet everyone around her was moving at a much quicker pace. She felt as though she was stuck in a bubble, watching the world happen around her while she stood perfectly still. A surreal feeling. Her mind just wouldn't let go of the events unfolding around her love affair. She decided to say a prayer to steady her mind. She recited the Hail Mary over and over. She kept praying, silently in her head, even as the meeting was beginning. She sat down at the conference table, not at the head of the table, which was her traditional seat. She just sat there, continuing to pray.

Finally, one of her coworkers tapped her on the shoulder several times. "Janet, are you okay?"

Janet snapped out of it, patted her coworker on the hand, and said, "Yes, yes of course. I'm fine. I just had a busy weekend and didn't get much sleep. Thank you. Now where were we?"

She got up and went to her normal spot at the head of the table to begin the morning meeting as if nothing had happened.

After the meeting as she got up, a wave of anxiety flooded back, overpowering her senses. She ducked into her office and clutched at her desk for a moment, breathing slowly and praying for calm. She then texted

Richard to tell him she was on her way, grabbed her purse, and headed out the door.

When she got into the car, she sat for a few minutes in complete silence. She felt on the verge of hyperventilation. She tried to concentrate on her breathing and nothing else. *In through the nose, out through the mouth, in through the nose, out through the mouth—*

Suddenly, her phone buzzed with a text message.

It was Curtis, reminding her he was going to be late coming home tonight. He was catering a dinner that was going to run very long into the evening.

With the realization that Curtis was going to be home late, she decided to text Sally and ask her to pick up her kids from school and take them to her house for the evening. She explained that she and Curtis were both going to be working late that evening. Sally agreed, with no questions asked.

Now that she had freed herself for the evening, she could get back to Richard, to discuss their plans for the future and what to do about Lily. She texted Richard and drove toward the rectory.

Her phone buzzed as Richard responded, *I'm preparing a special lunch just for you. Please try not to worry about Lily. I'll take care of her. Let's just enjoy our morning and afternoon together. I love you.*

Janet felt a wave of relief come over her, as if God Himself had lifted the burden from her shoulders. She looked up and said aloud, "Thank you God for giving me Your wonderful servant. He has truly opened my heart to what love really is, and I know you have spoken to him personally and shown him the way for our true happiness."

When she arrived at the rectory, she hit the button on the garage door opener Richard had given her the week prior, then drove, closing the door behind her.

As she got out of the car, Richard greeted her at the door with a broad smile, a kiss, and a lingering embrace. She could feel his erect penis against her thigh as they held one another, and she jokingly asked, "Is that a Rosary in your pocket or are you just happy to see me?" They both laughed as he led her into the house.

They walked hand in hand into the living room and sat on the couch beside one another. She could smell a wonderful aroma coming from the kitchen.

"What is that lovely smell?" she asked.

"Veal picatta. An elegant meal for an elegant lady." He reached up to push back a bit of hair from her face.

Janet smiled, and they began to kiss. Then the kissing grew intense, and petting led to fondling. Then Richard began stroking Janet's hair. Janet leaned against the back of the couch and said, "Richard, that feels good. I love the way you stroke my head and hair. I feel so sensual just from your touch."

Janet could smell on Richard's body a hint of the herbs and spices from his cooking. The scent was intoxicating and it added to her passion for him. The more he stroked her hair, the more aroused Janet felt. She reached between Richards legs and began stroking his erect penis. The sexuality between them was overwhelming as they began to make love.

Afterward, they got dressed and Janet lay down in Richard's lap. As he stroked her hair, Janet whispered the question that hung over them, "What are we going to do about Lily?"

"Please let me worry about Lily. I promise you I will take care of Lily."

With that said, no other word was spoken for a few minutes. Richard just continued stroking Janet's hair. Breaking the silence, he began to hum very softly. Janet felt the gentle vibration on Richard's chest, and it soothed her.

"Richard, I love you so very much."

"I love you too, my beloved."

Just then a timer went off in the kitchen. "The veal is ready" Richard said as he gently helped Janet up from the couch.

They went into the kitchen to plate the meal and they went into the dining room and nodded their heads in prayer before savoring their veal picatta and wine.

Janet thought to herself, *It's just as we had done a week ago when our love for one another had been declared before God.*

When lunch was over they cleaned up the dishes and the kitchen. Just as the last dish was put into the dishwasher, Janet reached into her purse and handed Richard the note that was left at her office.

He looked at it for what seemed to be only an instant, then folded it and put it in his front pocket saying, "I promise you Janet, this will be handled. Please don't worry. In fact, I have a little adventure planned for us today that will be just the thing to take our minds off all our trials and tribulations. We're going on a drive to White's Mountain. I've discovered the most beautiful spot on the top of the mountain that will take your breath away. It's only a forty-five minute drive from here. What do you say?"

Janet put her arms around Richard's neck and kissed him. "I say yes. I have all day to spend with you and I say we enjoy it. What a wonderful idea, Richard."

With that, they got into Richard's old Volvo and left for the mountain top.

As they drove away with anticipation, they failed to notice Lily, who'd been parked one street up the entire time they were together at the rectory.

She began to follow them.

5
INSTEAD, PERFECT LOVE CASTS OUT FEAR...

About forty-five minutes later, Richard and Janet arrived at an old barn in a clearing next to some pasture land. It was the only structure of any kind for miles. There was an old chimney about fifty yards away, obviously the only thing left from a fire from long ago. The barn was mostly grey from years of neglect. There were boards missing and the two large front doors were barely hanging onto their hinges. The barn was the marker for an old dirt road that would lead them to the secluded mountain-top destination Richard had planned for them.

He stopped at the old barn for a moment and paused in silence. He grabbed Janet by the hand, and she noticed a tear running down his cheek.

She reached over and rubbed the tear from his face. "What is it, my beloved? What's wrong?" she asked.

Richard stared deeply into her eyes, and answered, "I never thought I would find my true love again like I have found in you. You've opened my heart and I can't imagine how I could ever be without you. You are as beautiful as Heaven's own breath and as pure as Mother Mary herself. I want you to know that I will always love and never forsake you. This road we've chosen is going to be difficult for us, and it will be fraught with obstacles and hard decisions. My question to you is this. Is your love strong enough to handle what lies before us?"

Janet paused for a moment, took a deep breath and spoke in a soft secure tone, "Richard, I am forsaking my worldly life so that I might know the love we share. If I didn't know with every fiber of my heart that God Himself has brought us together, I wouldn't be here. Our bond is eternal. I did not know love like I know it with you. I promise you, no man, or woman, will ever come between our love. There are no obstacles large enough that our love cannot overcome." Then she leaned over and kissed him.

They sealed their pact with a tender squeeze of hands and a smile. Then Richard continued the two mile drive up the road to the secluded mountain top spot he had discovered.

When they arrived, they got out and stood for a moment enjoying the view. They were facing the valley below from a precipice. From their vantage point, they could see the entire town of Bridlewood. They stood silently by the edge as they absorbed the beauty before them. The majestic mountain range in the distance seemed to protect their small town, like the outstretched wings of an eagle. A mist hung just above the town. They could smell the freshness of the air around them. Leaves of every color blanketed the ground as if a golden carpet had been laid out just for them. They stood in each other's arms, as if nothing in the world even existed. A feeling of true security overwhelmed them both.

Richard then walked over to the car, pulled out a picnic basket from the trunk and began laying out a blanket.

"Richard, we just ate lunch an hour ago. There's no way I could possibly eat again."

Richard responded with a grin on his face, "Janet, this is not food for our bodies. This is food and drink for our immortal souls." He then began preparations for Holy Communion.

But neither one noticed that about a hundred yards away stood Lily.

She was perfectly camouflaged between two trees peering through her camera which sported a large telephoto lens.

Lily wasn't new to discreet surveillance. She'd picked up quite a few tricks during her time working for the FBI. She'd been retired for about ten years and was enjoying her job as the church secretary and assistant to the priest. It was a far cry from her former life, but it was also a good change of pace, and a peaceful way to live. She suffered from anxiety disorder and mild PTSD, so her life at the church was just the thing she needed to keep her calm and content. She had immersed herself in her faith and it brought her great comfort, until now.

She found herself not only upset with the knowledge that her priest had decided to break his vows of celibacy to the church, but also enraged by the fact that he chose to break those vows with a married parishioner in his flock. What made it worse for Lily was the fact that she was so fond of Curtis and Janet's children. As far as she could tell, they represented what most would call the ideal Catholic family.

She knew she had to do something about this inappropriate relationship. Lily wasn't yet sure what she was going to do with all this evidence, but she was gathering it because but she knew *something* had to be done. Lily was very good at hiding her feelings and compartmentalizing so she was confident she could continue as a good and faithful servant at her church for her priest, while still gathering necessary intelligence against Father Richard and Janet for the abomination they were perpetrating.

She felt her faith was being tested. She also believed it was her duty as a Catholic to help maintain the integrity of the church, so there she was, taking pictures and taking notes. She'd been observing them for quite some time and now the events of the past week had confirmed her suspicions. The relationship that Father Richard and Janet had cultivated was dangerous and it was highly inappropriate in the eyes of God, and in the eyes of Lily. As far as she was concerned, something had to be done. What that something was going to be however, was beyond her ability to know at this point. But Lily fully trusted in God. She knew He would reveal to her what would need to be done and when to do it.

In the meantime, Richard had laid out the consecrated bread and wine. They recited the Apostles' Creed, said three Hail Marys, and then recited the Lord's Prayer. After their prayers, Richard offered to Janet the bread and wine, and then Janet did the same for him. They each made the sign of the cross as they partook of the holy meal. Both prayed in silence after.

When they finished praying, Richard took Janet's hand and said to her, "I love you Janet."

Janet's eyes glistened, welling up with teary emotion, and she softly responded, "I love you too, Richard."

With only those words being spoken, they disrobed and made love once again. For Janet and Richard, every time they made love, they considered it a sacred and holy act for which God had given loving approval. An unspoken vow was shared between the two of them, and they took this vow more seriously than anything in their lives.

Afterward they lay naked and drifting off to sleep before this glorious view on an unseasonably warm day.

After watching the two sleep for about thirty minutes, Lily packed up her gear and headed to her truck. She'd parked behind the old barn at the base of the small dirt road. As she was hiking back, she reflected on the things she had observed between Father Richard and Janet, and then she began to pray, asking God for guidance.

When she arrived at her truck, she got into the cab and sat quietly, poised as though waiting for God's response to her plea. She closed her eyes and cleared her mind, like in a meditative state, then with almost a jerk, she snapped her eyes open and pulled out her phone.

She scrolled through the church directory she kept on her phone, and stopped at the names Curtis and Janet Sheffield. She punched in a number, and typed out a message: *Curtis, it is with a heavy heart that I must inform you of the affair between Father Richard and your wife, Janet. It pains me deeply to tell you this, but I feel it is my duty to do so. I will meet you at your restaurant at 4pm, exactly. I will sit by myself at a table and order a Rueben sandwich and a glass of Guinness. Come sit with me and I will explain.* Lily hit "send message" and it was on its way.

Seconds later, Curtis received the message. He didn't recognize the number but he opened it. Reading in disbelief, he fell heavily into a chair, turning pale and feeling slightly faint. He quickly responded, *"Who is this?"* but there was no response. It was now two. He had two hours to prepare for the mysterious liaison with the accuser of his wife and priest.

Meanwhile, Lily, intentionally ignoring Curtis's text, started her truck and headed for town. As she pulled out from behind the barn and onto the paved road, Father Richard's Volvo was parked at the end of the dirt road next to the old barn. Lily passed right by them and in a sudden panic of being discovered there, she accelerated.

Janet and Richard, catching sight of the truck, turned to one another. Janet blurted out, "Oh my God Richard, it's Lily. She's seen us. You have to catch her Richard. Hurry, hurry."

Richard echoed her distress, saying, "Dear God, we have to stop her."

He hit the accelerator as hard as he could, spinning the wheels of the Volvo and throwing dirt into the air behind him as he sped away.

By this time, Lily was doing at least fifty down the winding, narrow mountain road.

Richard was close behind, desperately trying to catch up to her. Janet clutched Richard's thigh as hard as she could with one hand and grasped the side of her seat with the other, trying to keep herself steady.

As Lily sped down the mountainous road, she approached a blind curve and began to lose control when she rounded the curve too quickly. The truck's rear slid out from under her, and as she turned the wheels in an attempt to correct the skid, the truck overcorrected and slid off the side of the road down a steep incline.

The truck flipped over several times, and Lily was thrown out. The truck landed with a gruesome crash against a large oak tree.

Richard and Janet stopped in the middle of the curve and rushed down.

The hill, littered with broken saplings and small trees, was very steep. They could hardly keep their balance as they descended. Janet got to Lily first.

Blood was gushing from Lily's forehead and a small sapling was sticking out of her side. She had impaled herself as she was thrown from the truck. She's lay about twenty feet from where the truck has crashed. Lily was barely conscious, and in severe pain.

Richard said, "We're going for help. Hold on Lily."

They began back up the steep incline and then Janet looked over toward the truck and saw the camera hanging by its strap on the side view mirror. In desperation of what might be on it, she went to the truck and grabbed it. She noticed Lily's notebook lying on the dash, with her name scribbled on the open page facing her.

She picked it up and began to read the details of the encounter she just shared with Richard. She gasped and cried out, "Richard, look what I've found."

She turned around to find Richard already reading the notebook over her shoulder. She hadn't even heard him walk up behind her. They both looked at each other with bewilderment, and then turned to Lily as she lie bleeding on the ground with an outstretched arm toward them.

"We'll be back with help, Lily. You'll be okay. Just hang on."

Richard grabbed the camera and notebook from Janet and said, "Let's go. Hold onto me." When got into the car, Janet reached for her phone to dial 911.

Richard grabbed her phone. "Wait a minute." He hesitated a moment with the phone in his hand, then looked intently at Janet. "Maybe we shouldn't call."

He added, "No one has passed by and no one has seen us on this mountain. So, no one knows where we are and no one witnessed Lily's accident. Maybe this is God's way of protecting us."

Janet stared back at him for a moment, then took her phone from Richard's hand. "I think you may be right." She paused, staring at the phone for a second, but then put the phone in her purse. A moment later, she clutched the phone again, but the feeling quickly passed as she nervously scanned the horizon.

Richard started the car and slowly drove down the mountain.

Not another word was spoken between them the rest of the way down. With every turn, they just seemed to fall deeper into silence. It seemed as though they could reach out and wisp away some of the suffocating tension that filled the car. Instead of discussing a plan or even attempting a conversation, they just sat stiffly and quietly, holding hands all the way back into the rectory garage. Once the garage door closed behind them, they turned to one another, and Richard softly whispered, "We will never again speak of the last thirty minutes of our lives. God has protected us in His own way, and we must trust Him to continue protecting the union that only He has ordained." He leaned over to place a brief, soft kiss on the corner of her mouth.

Janet gently nodded her head in agreement and they walked quietly into the house.

6
MY SOUL IS WEARY WITH SORROW;
STRENGTHEN ME...

The fog rolled in like a gentle blanket sent to comfort the weary. The coldness of the light rain that had started to fall was just enough to awaken Lily. She found it difficult to see through a thin stream of blood and dirt passing over her eyes. She took her hand, covered in blood as well, and tried to wipe her eyes. She was able to clear her vision enough to see her truck slammed against a tree ten feet from where she lay.

Regaining her bearing a bit, she tried to make sense of what had happened. She looked up the steep hill and realized no one could see her from the road. She knew it was unlikely that Richard and Janet were calling for help, nor would they return to rescue her. If she was going to survive, it was going to be up to her and her alone.

She tried to roll over to get into a more comfortable position because her side was burning like there was a flame coming from inside her. But when she tried to move, there was a shooting pain that went through her like she had only felt once before.

She recalled a time during an investigation twenty years earlier when she and her partner were on a routine stakeout involving organized crime. They had been sitting in her car when, out of nowhere, they heard gun fire. They fled the car to take cover. Once in position, they engaged the suspects, exchanged gunfire, and called for backup. They were surprised by the shooting, considering the stakeout was not considered a dangerous situation. After it was over and arrests were made, they began to assessed themselves for injuries.

Three suspects were dead and two had gunshot wounds. One of their own wounded was Lily's partner William, but everyone called him Steamboat. He'd been shot in the arm. They had become extremely close and she was the one tending to his wound.

He was going to be okay, but as Lily was dressing his wound, she'd realized her side was burning like someone had placed a burning match directly on her side. Lily had been shot as well. The bullet had gone straight through her, but the pain was excruciating when she reached down to stop the bleeding. With all of the adrenalin from the fire fight, she hadn't even realized she was shot.

It turned out the bullet ruptured her spleen and she was sent to the hospital for surgery. The doctors were able to repair the damage, and after a few weeks of recovery, Lily was able to return to her job.

The pain Lily now felt was reminiscent of that pain. She reached down and to her surprise, there was a sturdy sapling protruding from her side. Lily realized she'd been impaled and was precariously stuck to the ground by this small tree.

Luckily, Lily was dressed for the occasion. She was wearing the same utility pants she'd worn while training to become a field agent and she remembered her multitool in her side pocket. She reached into her pocket, but the multitool was not there. She frantically searched the other pocket, all the while the pain was increasing.

She realized being thrown from the truck must have thrown the multitool from her pocket as well. She began looking around. The ground was covered with leaves. The ground was damp so when she swept the leaves out of her way there was nothing but mud. It seemed an impossible task.

After about thirty minutes her hand brushed up against a piece of metal and she was able to retrieve, with just two fingers, her multitool. Lily felt a wave of relief that was soon overshadowed by the pain of her side.

Her eyesight was again blurred by blood that from the gash in her head. With all the pain in her side, she barely noticed that her head had a large gash from her ear to the top of her scalp. She opened her multitool and used the knife to cut her sleeve off and she used the sleeve to wrap her head to stop the bleeding. She now had to focus on how she was going to remove herself from this tree.

Lily took as deep a breath as she could and began to saw through the base of the sapling. It was excruciatingly painful and difficult to reach around behind her back and apply enough pressure to saw through it. The base of the sapling was only a couple of inches thick but for Lily it felt like a massive tree trunk and her progress was slow going. She had to stop and rest every minute or so. While resting, she opened her mouth to catch a fine mist of rain on her tongue, just a tease for her growing thirst.

After about an hour of sawing, she began to feel the sky spinning in her eyes. She grabbed the ground with both her hands, squeezing the mud between her fingers. She yelled as loud as she could, as if she were her own motivation, "Lily, *don't you dare pass out. You get your ass moving and don't let go. If you let go, you will die. Do you understand me Lily?*"

The personal pep talk seemed to work. Lily paused for a moment and then screamed, "*Yes ma'am, I will stay awake and finish my mission. God please help me.*"

She regained her composure and with just three more strokes of her blade felt the sapling's base crack, then split. The sapling finally gave way.

She rolled as far over as the tree's top would allow, buried her face in the mud, and began to wail in pain. She then mustered all of her strength and reached behind her, and with her teeth grinding on piece of tree limb, grabbed from the forest floor, and pulled the sapling out, feeling her flesh tear as the sapling exited her body.

Lily then took her other shirt sleeve and wrapped it around her body as tightly as she could to stop the bleeding.

After that, she fell to her back, with her knees in the air, allowing the rain to wash away the pain and agony. She kept her eyes open and it seemed she could feel every raindrop as it fell on her face and rolled down.

As she lay there, trying to regain some strength, she began to wonder if there was any chance that Richard and Janet really went for help. Surely the two of them, despite their personal behavior, wouldn't be so cruel and selfish that they would allow her to die out here, just to keep their secret.

Lily closed her eyes, pursed her lips and whispered to herself aloud, "Of course they left you to die. You're on your own out here. Now get up and save yourself. If you believe help is coming for you, then you are sadly mistaken. You have to push through the pain and save yourself. Don't let them win."

With that, Lily dug her hands into the mud and lifted herself off the ground. Then she began to scream. Not so much out of pain, but out of self motivation to force herself complete the arduous task of simply getting up.

As she stood up, she began to cry in relief. She was painfully limping, not realizing that her leg was burning in pain from her right thigh. She thought she must have cracked or fractured her thigh bone, but she knew she had to make her way to the cab of the truck. She ignored the pain and trudged on.

When she got to the truck, the door was open. She reached in and pulled the seat lever so she could push the back of the bench seat forward. It revealed a first aid kit, a gallon of water and a slightly dirty old towel. She grabbed all three, pushed the seat back to its upright position and she pulled herself up into the truck.

Lily first opened the water and drank as much as she could before she was forced to take a breath. She then grabbed the towel and cleaned off her face and arms. She opened the first aid kit, found some rubbing alcohol, untied the shirt sleeve from her side and began to pour it onto the two holes on her side. She screamed in agony and she beat on the dash with her fist as the pain of the alcohol on the open wounds shot through her entire body.

With a sudden, joyful awareness, she reached to open her glove box. Inside was a 9mm pistol, a flashlight and a bottle of whiskey. She reached for the whiskey and drank it as if it was water. Lily began to feel a slight sense of relief as she put her head back on the seat.

After about thirty minutes, Lily decided it was time to make her way up the steep incline and to the road, where she hoped she could find some help. It was getting late. She looked down at her watch. It was 6:30. She drank more water, hooked her gun to her belt, put the whiskey bottle and the flashlight in her pocket and carefully got out of the truck. She was in excruciating pain, but determined to make her way to the road.

She found a good walking stick among the broken limbs scattered around her as a result of the truck tumbling down the mountain. She slowly made her way, inch by inch it seemed, up the steep incline. She used the walking stick like a handle to pull the weight of her body upwards.

She continued this for over an hour, taking a break every couple of minutes it seemed. Her strength was fading as quickly as the sunlight around her. She kept telling herself, with every step she took, "You can do this Lily, you can do this. Don't let them win."

As eight o'clock arrived, and darkness fell upon her, Lily finally reached the top. The road was finally beneath her feet. She looked across the road and saw a rock overhang that would shield her from the rain and give her a safe place to rest while she waited for someone to pass by.

She slowly crossed the road and found a tree stump that someone had created to be a seat. Off to the side of the stump, on the adjacent rock face, was a spout pouring mountain spring water out onto the edge of the road. Lily felt as though she'd just won the lottery.

She sat on the stump, with her walking stick leaned against the bank beside her, and waited. A misty fog was rising from the road before her, and as she watched the fog float gently over the asphalt, all she could do was wait and wonder to herself, *God, please don't let me die, sitting here on this stupid stump.*

7
THEY EXCHANGED THEIR GLORIOUS GOD FOR SOMETHING DISGRACEFUL...

Janet was sitting quietly at the dining room table in the rectory, Richard was in the kitchen opening a bottle of wine. She had her phone in her hand as she stared at the blank screen. She was nervously waiting for Richard to say the words that would make what happened have some meaning, words that could justify what they had done.

She kept running the recent events through her mind, thinking about how her life had been turned inside out. She knew her life was now in a place from which there was no turning back.

She lowered her head and softly whispered to herself, "God, please give me a sign that leaving Lily to die is part of your plan for me and Richard. I promise I will not forsake your shephard and vessel. Richard is your good and faithful servant, and I promise to serve him as I serve you. I promise to let your will be done, but please give me the strength of mind to follow it."

Janet looked up to find Richard standing before her with his head lowered in prayer with her. In one hand was a glass of chardonnay and in the other was a double shot of scotch. He looked up and, as their eyes met, he made the sign of the cross on himself and sat down beside her.

He reached for Janet's hand and as she placed her hand into his, he gave a little squeeze. Then they began to discuss dinner plans. After all, they did have the rest of the evening to themselves.

"I think I have some steaks in the fridge and I can steam some broccoli in the new bamboo steamer I just had delivered last week. I've been wanting to use it and now I have the opportunity to do so."

"That would be wonderful," she responded.

"Your wish is my command, my beloved" he said as he kissed her hand.

Janet smiled and leaned in for a kiss. When their lips met, Janet felt a chill down her spine, then a wave of peace came over her that she hadn't felt since the first time they had made love in the little prayer room. She closed her eyes, smiled and silently prayed, "Thank you Lord God. I have received your sign."

Richard then got up from the table, took Janet's hand and led her to the bedroom. He took out his phone and put it into a speaker dock. Frank Sinatra began to croon, as Richard pulled Janet to him and for a slow dance in front of the bed. As they slowly twirled, Janet noticed a picture on the dresser of Richard's late wife and him on their wedding day. She hadn't noticed it before. She said in a soft, loving tone, "Your wife was beautiful."

"She was, but not nearly the beauty I now have in my life, in my embrace. You take my breath away every time I see you, and it pains me not to be able to walk up to you and take you into my arms and kiss you. But I know that God has a plan for us and he'll reveal it in his own time."

As the music continued, they stopped dancing and undressed. While serenaded by the velvety lyrics of Sinatra's "My Way," they made love.

Later, they fell asleep, spooning one another.

They had only been asleep for about an hour when Janet began to dream about the two of them on the mountain top. They were having communion, just as before, when suddenly Lily stood before them. She was covered in blood, and with her hand outstretched, pointed directly at Janet, "You will not forsake my God with the abomination the two of you have become."

Janet jerked herself upright in the bed, threw her hands to her chest, and began breathing with shallow, quick breaths. She didn't say a word. She didn't want to wake Richard. She slowly slid out of bed and put on Richard's robe which was hanging on the bedpost.

She went to the kitchen, opened the refrigerator door and pulled out the bottle of Chardonnay. She grabbed a wine glass from the cabinet and gave herself a large pour. She then walked into the living room and sat down on the couch. She was quietly drinking the wine, trying desperately not to think about what they had done to Lily, when the doorbell rang.

Janet's heart leapt to her throat. She frantically jumped up and scurried into the bedroom to find Richard groggily getting dressed and looking at his watch. He said to Janet, "Get dressed. I completely forgot I had a meeting with Cindy about the upcoming youth program. Stay here, and I'll let her know I can't meet with her today."

Janet could faintly hear Richard open the front door and begin talking to Cindy. She couldn't make out what they were saying, so she took off Richard's robe and got dressed. She could still hear Richard and Cindy talking, but now they were in the foyer of the house.

Janet began to pace about in the bedroom. She walked over to the dresser and picked up the picture of Richard and his late wife. She was amazed at the similarities between herself and his wife. They both had blonde hair and blue eyes. Though the picture was over thirty years old, she noticed that they had basically the same hairstyle as well. They both shared similar facial structure and they both had the same small bump on their noses. Janet thought to herself, "We could be sisters. Almost identical twins."

Janet shook her head and returned the picture to the dresser. She then noticed a wooden box sitting beneath the picture. Her curiosity got the best of her and she opened it. Inside were a few old letters, a rosary, a couple of watches and what was obviously Richard's and his wife's wedding bands.

She picked up the old letters, but noticed underneath the letters was a phone. Seemingly fresh dirt was smeared on the screen. Janet picked it up and noticed the USMC emblem on the case. She recognized it immediately as Lily's. Richard must have picked it up at the scene of the accident. Janet turned the power on. Surprisingly, it came on and didn't require a passcode.

Janet began to browse through the phone. She looked through the pictures and found pictures of Lily with people Janet had never seen before. Mostly they were men with hats with various FBI insignias on them. They were obviously people from Lily's days in the FBI. There were a few screenshots of guns and ammunition. Janet had no idea Lily was so hardcore about these sorts of things. Lily was not exactly sociable, but she always seemed docile to Janet.

Janet moved onto the call log. There wasn't anything surprising there. A few calls to the church and some other random names that Janet did and didn't recognize. Then she went into Lily's messages and that's where she saw the last message Lily sent. It was to Curtis. Janet recognized the number and then she read what it said. "Oh God!" she cried out, then immediately covered her mouth, realizing she had spoken aloud and hoped she wasn't heard.

Janet put the phone down on the dresser and hurried to the bedroom door. She placed her ear against the door so she could hear the conversation between Richard and Cindy. She could hear Richard leading her to the front door and telling her goodbye. When Janet heard the front door close, she opened the bedroom door to find Richard walking toward her. "Did she hear me?"

"She heard it, but she didn't say anything. She looked a little puzzled, so I just hurried her out of the house."

"We have a bigger problem than that Richard. Come with me." She led him to the dresser. "I apologize for going through your things, but I found Lily's phone, which you obviously picked up at the accident. Look at this." She showed him the text message to Curtis.

"We need a plan Richard, and we need it now," she begged.

Richard slowly led Janet by the hand to the living room couch. He sat her down and calmly stated, "Lily never made it to that meeting and we have all of her evidence. As far as Curtis knows, it could be some disgruntled parishioner at the church just trying to stir up trouble because we've become such close friends. You know there are those within this church who don't like that I was formerly married. We don't need a plan. There's nothing to do. I know it's a lot to take in and we have been through an arduous day, but we must stay the course Janet, and remember that God is in charge. He will protect us and guide us. *We must trust in Him.*"

Janet slowly nodded her head in agreement, and Richard said, "Good. Now, let's fix a nice dinner and let the worries of the day pass us by."

8
IF A MAN IS FOUND LYING WITH THE WIFE OF ANOTHER MAN...

After dinner, Richard and Janet faced the fact that she was going to have to go home to her family. The question that burned on both their minds, yet neither spoke aloud, was whether or not Curtis was going to tell Janet about the mysterious text he received earlier that day.

Richard walked Janet to her car, which was parked in the garage, and as they kissed goodbye, Richard said, "Don't forget that God is in charge. Let Him guide you, and keep the presence of mind to let Curtis guide the conversation. Don't admit to anything if he accuses you of infidelity. Tell him he's wrong, and tell him to call me. I'll help him understand that your being unfaithful is not possible."

Janet paused for a moment and after a look of bewilderment, agreed. "Okay Richard. I will trust in God, and in you. I love you."

Richard opened the garage door and Janet backed out and drove away. Richard closed the garage door behind her and walked back into the house, rubbing his hands up and down on his face. He made his way to the prayer room and lay prostrate before the crucifix. He felt closer to God before the altar, as if he were being intimate with the Holy Spirit. The feeling he got from it was euphoric and gave him a sense of belonging. Much like the feeling he got while lying with Janet. He prayed for the rest of the evening.

As Janet was heading home, she called her friend Carol, who had the children. Janet pulled up Carol's driveway and they all met her at the car. "Thank you so much for watching the children, Carol. You're an angel."

The children got into the car and they headed for home. They spent the fifteen minute drive home discussing the events of their day at school.

Janet asked the children, "How was your day? Did you see Father Richard? Don't you feel he's a wonderful priest?"

The children just looked at her and said nothing.

She added wistfully, "We're so blessed to have him in our church and in our lives."

The children shrugged their shoulders and began to dig through their book bags to show their mother their classwork.

When they got home Curtis's car was in the driveway. He wasn't expected until after eleven. Janet felt her stomach turn, and she took a deep breath as they got out of the car and made their way to the front door.

The children ran ahead calling for their father as they opened the door. Curtis came to greet them in the foyer, and he gathered them into bear hugs as they ran through the front door.

As she walked into the house Janet noticed Curtis walking back toward the dining room table with a glass of whiskey in his hand. He had greeted the children with love and excitement, like there was nothing wrong at all. Curtis asked the children if they'd eaten and finished their homework. They had, so Curtis told the children they could head to the recreation room and play video games. They jumped up and down, and again gave their father a big hug and scampered away.

Janet walked up to Curtis and leaned in to give him a kiss, but he pulled away. "What's wrong Curtis? Weren't you supposed to cater a dinner tonight? I wasn't expecting you until later tonight."

Curtis held his phone with the screen facing her. He handed it to Janet and said with his jaws clenched tightly, "Would you care to explain this text?"

Janet read what Lily had written and scoffed, "You've got to be kidding me. How could someone possibly say something like that to you? Whoever it is, they are demented and mean. I would *never* cheat on you Curtis, and especially with Father Richard. A sad look fell over her face. She reached for Curtis to give him a hug, but he pulled away from her. Janet, filled with a mixture of emotions, found it easy to shed a tear. "For Christ's sake, who could be so cruel as to accuse me of having an affair with our priest? Well, who was it? What did they say to you when they got to your restaurant?"

Curtis' shoulders dropped as he slowly shook his head. "Whoever it was never showed up. I waited for two hours. I finally sent the guys to do the catering job without me and I waited for another hour, just in case. I'm not sure what to believe, so I came home to wait for you and the kids. Why would anyone send that to me and then not show up?"

"Only someone who is jealous of our friendship with Father Richard. Why don't you call him and talk to him about it. I'm sure he could explain that this is nothing more than an attempt to shame him because they don't like him. You know as well as I that there are a lot of people at that church who are actively trying to get rid of him for nothing more than the fact that he's been married. Closed-minded, ignorant people, at that."

Curtis thought for a moment and said, "Maybe you're right, Janet. But what am I supposed to do?"

Janet looked Curtis straight in the eye and said, "Call Father Richard and speak with him. You know him. You know the idea of my having an affair with him is an impossibility. *Please call him.* If nothing else, you could sit down with him and have a drink and a cigar, and discuss it. I promise it'll make you feel better. Please, Curtis."

"Maybe I will. Maybe I will," Curtis said with a sigh of relief in his voice.

Janet grabbed Curtis's phone and handed it to him. "No. Call him now."

Curtis walked out the front door as he called. "Father Richard, this is Curtis. Do you have a minute?"

Janet sat down at the dining room table, lowered her head, and began to silently pray. She desperately wanted to follow Curtis outside so she could hear the conversation between her husband and her lover, but she recalled the words that Richard had told her. But she restrained herself.

She decided she should occupy herself with something, anything, to take her mind away from what was happening. She went into the kitchen to rearrange the spice rack. It was a ridiculous task, but putting the spices in alphabetical order kept her mind off everything else. She found the trivial task to be eerily comforting.

In fact, Janet got so caught up in the organization that she didn't notice Curtis standing right beside her. Curtis took her hand and said, "You're right sweetheart. I think I might be overreacting. I'm going to the rectory. Father Richard has invited me over for a drink. And he's offered to counsel me about my anxiety over this crazy anonymous text, to help me see just how ridiculous the accusation is. I'll be back in a little while."

Janet could feel her face starting to warm and flush. She feared this might betray her, so she leaned in to hug him. As calmly as she could muster, she said, "I'm glad he was able to make you feel better. I'll see you when you get back." Turning from him, and nervously brushing her hair back from her face, she added with a sigh, "I'll probably go to bed. It's been a stressful day. Love you."

With that, Curtis grabbed his keys off the key hook next to the front door and left.

Janet walked to the window, peeled back a corner of the curtain and peered out as Curtis got into his green Jeep Cherokee and drove away. She stood staring out the window for a few more moments, then realized her sight had homed in on the area down the street where she'd seen Lily's truck just the night before. Her eyes began to well up with tears, then suddenly she let go of the curtain, straightened her posture, and wiped the tears from her eyes with a sniffle.

She started for the bedroom, but then paused, turned around, and went into the kitchen to begin emptying the cabinets. She vigorously cleaned them and organized everything that went back into them.

As Curtis drove up to the rectory, he saw that the front porch light was on. He pulled into the driveway and just sat in the Jeep for a few minutes, running over the events of the day. He was unsettled, his heart and mind battling it out in a search for truth.

Finally, he walked to the front door, and there was Father Richard, greeting him with a hug and a glass of whiskey.

"Welcome Curtis. I know it's been a stressful day for you, so please come on in and let's relax for a bit. I think you'll find this whiskey to your liking." With a wink, he added, "It's a fifteen year old single malt Scotch I've been saving for a special occasion, but tonight it seemed appropriate to share it with you." He placed his hand on Curtis' shoulder. "We'll sit outside on the back patio, if that's all right with you. I've started the gas fire pit. It'll keep the chill off."

Curtis thanked Father Richard for the whiskey, took a gulp, and followed him outside. There were five outdoor chairs that looked very comfortable. Several side tables sat between them. Three wind chimes were lightly blowing in the breeze. They made a peaceful chiming that harmonized, as if an invisible conductor was bringing them together into a sweet, soothing melody. It put Curtis at ease.

Father Richard directed Curtis to one of the chairs and sat down beside him. On the table between them was a lead crystal ashtray and two Cuban cigars—gifts from a parish member who'd specifically asked Father Richard to remain anonymous, since, of course, Cuban cigars are illegal.

The two men began their conversation with simple small talk about the weather and then Father Richard asked to see the text message. Curtis pulled it up and handed the phone to Father Richard.

Father Richard took the phone, read the message, and deleted it.

"What the hell did you do that for?" Curtis yelled. "I was planning on trying to find out whose number that was and confront them.

Father Richard put his hand on Curtis's shoulder and calmly said, "Curtis, my brother, you don't want to do that. The only reason you want to do that is to prove to yourself that Janet isn't having an affair with her priest. You already know in your heart that this is not the case. Look me in the eye Curtis. I am *not* having an affair with your wife. Your wife is not having an affair with anyone. She loves and cherishes you and your children.

"Your family is the example I use when I counsel other married couples who are having a tough time in their marriages. And let's not forget that I'm a priest who's bound by Church doctrine to remain celibate. I've made a promise to God Himself and the Pope to honor my priesthood and the Church."

He leaned over toward Curtis. "And Curtis, I also hope you know that I'm your dear friend and brother. I would never do that to you.

"Most importantly, Janet would never do that to you, nor would she betray her own Church in such a disgraceful manner. She's better than that, and you know it."

He pointed to the phone. "To keep a record of that shameful text would only disgrace the sanctity of the marriage vows you and Janet have shared for twenty-five years. You have more honor than that, Curtis. I know you do, because you're an honorable man, and you're better than that."

He leaned back in his chair, took a sip of whiskey, and said, "Turn the other cheek my friend, turn the other cheek. I don't think I need to tell you who said that."

"No you don't Father Richard, no you don't. Thank you."

Curtis gulped down the rest of his Scotch, took a deep breath, and asked, "Father Richard, will you hear my confession?"

Father Richard looked at Curtis, and tilted his with curiosity, because he knew Curtis had never asked him for confession in all the time he had been his priest. He put his glass on the edge of the table, and placed a hand on Curtis's head. "I would be honored my son."

"Bless me Father, for I have sinned" Curtis began. "It has been ten years since my last confession. I have chosen not to go to confession all this time because I didn't feel worthy of forgiveness." He dropped his head for a moment before continuing, "In my business, I meet many people, and many extremely beautiful women who are dressed at their best for whatever occasion I might be catering. Often, they hand me their phone numbers. I'm ashamed to say that on occasion, I've indulged in my sexual desires with some of them."

Curtis desperately looked for some understanding or empathy from Father Richard, but Father Richards only picked up his whiskey glass and held it in his hands.

Curtis continued, "I'm not proud of the affairs I've had, but I guess I did it because I was lonely at the time. Janet and I haven't had a very active sex life since our oldest child was born. That was fifteen years ago. She suffered from postpartum depression and it took her a long time to come out of it.

"We've always been happy together; it's just the sex life we once shared no longer seems an integral part of our lives. We do have sex, but not very often. And when we do, it's without any passion, almost as if she's checking off a box in her to-do list. But I've told her I'm okay with our sex life, and she's never questioned my loyalty.

"Father, I'm repentant of the sins I''ve perpetrated on my marriage, but I just couldn't help myself. It hasn't happened in a long time and I've vowed never to do it again, but I feel as though it's come between Janet and me in some way that I just can't see. But I can feel it."

Father Richard sat quietly listening, staring into the whiskey glass cradled between his hands.

Curtis helped himself to another glass of whiskey. "I've also been having some troubles with the restaurant itself. Business hasn't been as good as it once was and I am finding myself spending a lot of our savings and credit cards to keep the business afloat. I've lost a few employees and I've had to spend more time with the business, which hasn't helped our marriage. It's getting to a point where I'm only home on Sundays, and I'm exhausted from working all week.

"But I've always taken great pride in the fact that Janet picked up my slack and was the better parent, although recently I've felt Janet drift away and she's spending less and less time with the children and me. She says it's work, and that the church is keeping her so busy, but I'm afraid she may actually be having an affair. Not with you of course, but I really feel as though she *is*. And that text message just confirmed those feelings. Please forgive me."

Father Richard paused for a few moments and said, "You are forgiven, my son. God has washed away your sins. Go and sin no more."

He lifted his glass, took a sip, and added, "But I'm afraid I'll have to ask you to talk to your wife and proclaim these sins against her and God, and your marriage. It is God's will. Now, say three *Hail Marys*, two *Our Fathers* and the *Act of Contrition*. I absolve you of your sins."

Father Richard motioned the sign of the cross, Curtis responded in kind, and they hugged one another.

Curtis wiped a tear from his eye and said, "Thank you Father Richard, but..." He slowly shook his head "...you want me to tell Janet? Are you sure that's such a good idea? I mean, I'm not doing it anymore, and what's to gain by telling her?"

"Curtis, this is the only way your marriage will heal. I happen to know, with certainty, that your wife loves and cherishes you. With my guidance and counsel through these muddy waters, I'll help get the two of you through this. Trust me. I'm your priest and your shepherd. I would never allow harm to come to one of my flock.

With an air of authority and finality, he said, "Now. Let's have another drink and not speak of this again tonight. Let's just enjoy a pleasant evening.

"I've always loved the smell of the air after a good hard rain. It's as if God Himself has cleansed the Earth of it's sins in Holy Baptism. Here's to a fresh start and a new beginning."

The two tapped their glasses together in a toast and took a sip of whiskey. They then begin to smoke cigars, lighting them with matches and twirling them in their mouths as if performing a grand ritual. Father Richard put on some music and they both sat back and relaxed.

After about an hour and two more glasses of whiskey, Curtis excused himself to use the restroom. As he walked down the hallway to the bathroom, he happened to catch a glimpse of Father Richard's bedroom. The door was open about halfway. He wasn't looking for anything in particular, but he was curious to see what his priest's bedroom looked like. He thought to himself that it couldn't be different than anyone else's bedroom, but it did pique his interest to see how a *holy man of God* would arrange his bedroom.

Curtis pushed the door open a bit more. It looked like a normal bedroom to him and, as he shrugged his shoulders in slight disappointment, a brief glimmer from under the bed caught his eye. It was an earring.

Since the earring looked so out of place, Curtis reached down to pick it up and examine it.

He recalled it as an exact match to the David Yurman earrings he'd purchased for Janet's birthday only a month earlier. Curtis suddenly heard a noise from outside. It was probably a branch of the tree rubbing against the window, but it startled him.

He turned to make sure Father Richard was still on the back porch. He couldn't see the porch from where he was standing, but Father Richard was nowhere in sight.

Curtis shoved the earring in his pocket, put the bedroom door exactly the way it was, and proceeded to the bathroom.

Returning to the back porch, Curtis said, "Father Richard, thank you so much for a wonderful evening, but I think it's time I get back home to Janet. The Scotch and the cigars were amazing. And I appreciate your hearing my confession, but I'd still like to think about confessing to Janet. Let me pray on it, and I'll let you know what I decide. Is that okay with you?"

"Of course it is Curtis. After all, it's your decision. I can only guide you as I feel is necessary."

Father Richard led Curtis to the front door and the two men briefly hugged each other.

As Curtis was getting into his Jeep, Father Richard said, "God bless you Curtis, and give my love to Janet and the children."

"Will do, Father."

Curtis felt an urgency to get home. He couldn't reconcile the fact that he'd just found what looked like Janet's earring under Father Richard's bed. He tried to tell himself it *wasn't* Janet's. He had to find the earrings in Janet's jewelry box.

He spoke out loud to himself as he pulled into the driveway, "Please be two earrings in the jewelry box. Please be two earrings..."

Curtis opened the front door expecting Janet to be in bed. But she was still in the kitchen putting everything back into the cabinets.

Janet was startled to see him. "I didn't hear you come in, Curtis. How did it go with Father Richard?" She felt her insides trembling, and hoped Curtis couldn't see her anxiety.

"He made me feel a lot better. I'm sorry I got so upset earlier. You've been busy." "I just felt like the kitchen needed a deep cleaning. I'm almost finished. Why don't you go on to bed? I'll be along soon."

She walked over to Curtis and kissed him. "I'm glad Father Richard was able to help. It's a shame that someone could be so cruel as to stir up turmoil between us and besmirch our priest."

Curtis nodded his head saying, "I'll see you shortly."

Curtis made his way to the kid's bedrooms to make sure they were sleeping. And then went into his and Janet's bedroom, shut the door, and straight for Janet's walk-in closet. He headed for the cherrywood jewelry box in the corner. It stood about four feet tall, with ten drawers and little French doors that revealed all her necklaces.

He opened the top of the jewelry box to reveal at least fifty pairs of earrings. He took the earring out of his pocket. In the middle of the earring was a huge Ruby. He looked back into the jewelry box, carefully scanning back and forth trying to find the match. Finally, about two thirds down the rows of earrings, there it was. One single earring, a perfect match to one that Curtis held between his thumb and forefinger.

His stomach rose into his throat, and he felt the blood drain from his face. He stared at the earring in the box for a moment as the revelation sunk in, then he shut the jewelry box lid, tucking the earring he'd found back into his pocket, and went to bed.

8
"YOU WILL NOT CERTAINLY DIE," SAID THE SERPENT TO THE WOMAN...

The rain was pouring down so hard by mid afternoon, Lily could barely see anything outside of the rock overhang that was keeping her somewhat dry. She was weak, bleeding from her head and her side, and she wasn't sure how long she was going to remain conscious.

She heard a faint hum further up the mountain. With senses suddenly on high alert, she tilted her head to discern what was approaching. As the noise grew louder and closer, she recognized what sounded like the engine of a large truck. She put her left hand on the stump and her right hand on the rock face beside her.

She managed to get up and make her way to the middle of the road. She was dazed and confused, but she knew if she didn't stand in the road she wouldn't be seen. She knew she ran the risk of being run over and killed because the driver might not see her in time.

She didn't care. If she didn't try, she was going to die regardless.

As the truck approached she took out the flashlight with her right hand hoping to get attention. The truck came closer, she heard a loud horn so close she could feel the vibration. It was happening in slow motion for her and each millisecond felt like an eternity. She heard the brakes squeaking and the tires sliding, as the truck gripped the road through the wet asphalt. As the truck struck her, she was thrown backwards she prayed, "Dear God, let me live!" Then, everything went black.

Lily awoke to the sound of beeping and a woman's voice in the background. She felt groggy, but she was finally able to open her eyes to a pleasant, slightly plump, dark-haired nurse looking at her with a broad smile. As her eyes adjusted, Lily saw her name tag, *Hannah*.

Nurse Hannah, who reminded Lily of her own sweet grandmother, asked, "How are you feeling?"

She patted Lily's leg with a maternal tenderness. "You've been through quite an ordeal, Honey."

Lily blinked a couple of times. "What—"

Can you tell me your name?"

"My name... My name is... I can't remember my name." Lily grew agitated.

"Where am I? Is this a hospital?" She began to pull on her IV line as she tried to get up.

The nurse put a hand over the IV line to prevent Lily from yanking it out. "Calm down, Honey. Let's take this one step at a time."

As the nurse continued to calm Lily, a doctor came into the room with Lily's file. The doctor's presence filled the room with an air of authority, and a stunning beauty. She was a tall woman with long red hair tied in back and hanging down over her left shoulder. She asked the nurse for an update about Lily's injuries and mental state. Once satisfied, she introduced herself as Dr. Light.

Then she began to probe her with questions.

"Can you remember anything about what happened to you?"

Lily brow furrowed as she tried to recall. "A car accident, I think. I think I was in an accident. I remember tumbling down a mountain."

"Very good. Do you remember anything else?"

"Yes, yes... I was driving my truck down a mountain and someone ran me off the road. I rolled down the mountain and slammed into a tree."

Where did this happen?"

Lily shook her head in frustration, "I'm not sure. I'm having trouble remembering. I'm sorry."

"That's okay." Dr Light nodded. "Let's stop here."

Dr. Light turned to the nurse. "Give her some more pain medication and let's try again later." Looking back at Lily, "Get some rest."

The doctor smiled at Lily and Lily responded, managing a slight smile in return as she fell asleep.

Dr Light turned back to the nurse and said, "Call the detective and have him come down here."

"Yes, Doctor."

"She may be able to remember more, now that she is starting to come around."

Three hours later, Lily woke up, only this time the nurse, the doctor, and a man who looked like he was holding some kind of police badge in his hand were standing beside her bed.

Lily had regained her memory, and recalled everything that occurred on that mountain, but she wasn't planning to reveal that nugget to anyone. No, she wanted to wait until she'd decided what to do, given the unusual circumstances.

The police officer, who identified himself as detective Brown, stated that he had a few questions for her about what had led her to end up in the hospital.

Lily responded to every question with the same response. "I can't recall anything that happened after I found myself tumbling down the mountainside."

Detective Brown said, "The man who brought you to the hospital saved your life, but all he knew was that he found you lying on the side of the road on the outskirts of the city. He took me to the scene, but there was no evidence of any kind there."

"I don't remember that."

"Is there *anything* else you can remember?"

Lily apologized over and over again for not being able to recall what had happened and after thirty minutes of questioning, detective Brown said he would come back later and try again. After the detective and the doctor left the room, Lily had a few questions for the nurse. "What hospital am I in? What town am I in?

The nurse answered, "You're at Grey Hospital in Florence, South Carolina."

"How long have I been here?"

"You've been here for five days, in a medically induced coma so you could recover. We're all amazed that you survived, given the extent of your injuries. Honey, you're what we call a medical miracle."

"What about the man who dropped me off?"

"He wasn't able to shed any light as to what happened to you. He said he found you on the side of the road outside of the city and he only dropped you off because you were bleeding and looked near death. Do you remember any of that, Honey?"

Lily shook her head.

"Detective Brown was hoping you could shed a little light on what really happened to you."

The nurse reached into her pocket, and pulled out a picture. "This is the truck. Do you recognize it?" she asked, handing it to Lily.

Lily looked up at the nurse, shook her head and said, "I wish I could help you, but I really have no recollection of what happened to me. Maybe if

I rest some more, it will begin to come back to me. I'm so tired."

She patted Lily on the leg. "I'll be by to check on you later."

After the nurse left, Lily reached for the phone and dialed an old friend from her FBI days that happened to live in Florence. She had his number memorized from years of working with him, and after only three rings there was an answer.

"Hello." His deep, warm voice, with its southern drawl, was comforting, as it always reflected the heart of a caring yet resolute partner.

"Hey, Steamboat. This is Easter Lily." *Easter Lily* is what her FBI friends used to call her.

Steamboat was William Patterson's nickname because he'd grown up on the banks of the Mississippi river and loved watching the steamboats pass him by as a child.

Steamboat responded with concern, "Lily, what's goin' on with you? I haven't heard from you in fifteen years."

"Steamboat, I'm at Grey Hospital and I need you to come to the front door right now. Don't ask any questions. I'll fill you in on all the details when you get here. Can you do this for me?"

With no questions asked, Steamboat agreed, "Yes ma'am. I'll be there in twenty minutes. I'm in a red Toyota truck. Be lookin' for me."

"Thank you Steamboat. I'll be waiting for you."

Lily carefully removed her IV lines, grabbed a wheelchair from outside her door, and wheeled her way to the exit of the hospital. She only waited outside the hospital's front doors for a short time when she saw Steamboat pill up to the curb.

Lily painstakingly got into the front seat, with Steamboat's assistance. "Steamboat, get me out of here!"

Steamboat hit the gas. "What in the hell happened to ya, Lily? Why were you in the hospital, and why did you have me come snap you?"

Lily looked at the picture of the truck the nurse had given her. "Steamboat, I'll fill you in on the details about everything, but right now I'd like to go to your house.

Steamboat nodded in agreement.

Lilly added, "We have some work to do, but we need to get to a secure location. So please, no more questions yet."

"Yes ma'am. We'll be home in five minutes."

As Steamboat pulled into his garage, he asked Lily, "Okay, what's this all about?"

"Wait until we get inside."

As Lily and Steamboat entered his home from the garage Lily looked him straight in the eye and said, "Two people tried to kill me last week and I am going to expose them for all of their misdeeds even if it takes my last breath to do it."

"Tell me what ya need from me and I'll help any way I can. I'm with ya Lily. Always have been and always will be."

Lily put her hand on top of his, gave a little squeeze of acknowledgement and smiled, saying, "Thank you. I knew I could count on you, my friend."

Lily laid out their first steps. "I'm going to need you to go to the store for me to get a few things. I'll make a list. And I'll need access to your computer."

With that, she and her friend sat down at his old fifties style kitchen table. It was blue with aluminum tubing supports.

Steamboat bragged and said, "How do ya like my table and chairs, Lily? I found them at a local flea market, only fifty bucks.

Lily managed a small chuckle, saying, "You always were a cheap bastard."

They both laughed.

Lily sat down with a small sigh. "I appreciate you trying to lighten the mood for me. You've always been a true friend, and the only person who really understood me. Now we have some important work to do. Get us some coffee please."

Steamboat made the coffee, then gathered his laptop, a piece of paper, and a pen for Lily.

Lily took a sip of coffee and, as she lifted the cup, she felt a sharp pain in her side. She pulled up her hospital gown and asked Steamboat to look at it. He could clearly see the staples on the two wounds on her torso.

"They seem to be healing," Steamboat said. "Now to tell me what happened, Lily."

Lily told the whole story, and afterwards she began to make her list.

"That's one the most bizarre series of events I've ever heard, Lily." Steamboat said as she wrote. "We'll make that son-of-a-bitch priest pay for what he's done to you, and to that poor family."

Steamboat took the completed list and headed out to get what she needed, which included clothes, shoes, a cell phone and some personal items.

When he'd left, Lily opened the laptop computer and hacked into the FBI's database. Her time as an FBI analyst afforded her the necessary skills to easily find the mysterious person who dropped her off five hours away from her home. In less than ten minutes, referring to the photograph the nurse had given her, she was able to match the license plate number to a vehicle, and then track the vehicle to a name and an address. She researched the man's background and occupation: He was a trucker. Lived in a nice neighborhood. Recently divorced. The man had no record. He appeared to be an unassuming person with no obvious reason to lie about where he'd found Lily. Lily wondered, *Why would he have risked my life to drive me five hours from where he picked me up?*

When Steamboat got home, Lily was asleep on the couch. He got a blanket, put it over her, and sat in his recliner beside her as she slept for a few hours.

When Lily woke up, she asked Steamboat to examine her again. "Am I able to travel?"

Steamboat assures her, "You're going to be in some pain, but yes, in a day or two I believe you will be strong enough to travel."

"I need to find the man who brought me here, and then I need to go back home and deal with my so-called priest."

" I'll make sure ya eat well, and I have plenty of pain medication and antibiotics on hand to get ya fixed up. Don't you worry one bit, Easter Lily. I can handle it."

Lily smiled, "I knew I could count on old Steamboat Willie. Now let's eat. I'm starving. What kind of chow have you got around here?"

Steamboat got up, went into the kitchen and cooked some steaks he'd picked up while he was at the store earlier. They ate their meal together and spent the evening reminiscing about their days together in the Marines.

Steamboat spent the next few days caring for Lily as she got her strength back. After three days, he removed her staples and bandaged the wound, taking great care so her journey home would be as comfortable as possible.

The morning they were preparing to leave, Lily asked for a weapon.

Lily said, "Steamboat, we don't really know what this Brandon character is going to do when he sees me. We don't know why he chose not to take me to the nearest hospital and why he lied to the police about where he found me. We need to be prepared for anything."

Steamboat complied, but insisted, "You're still weak, so let me take point."

Lily nodded in agreement and they left the house to head to the home of Brandon Gates, Lily's mysterious savior.

The attractive, but unassuming ranch style house was situated in a middle-class neighborhood. As they pulled into the driveway, they noticed a tractor portion of a tractor-trailer parked behind the house. There was an F-350 diesel truck in the driveway. In her head, Lily could recall the sound of the diesel engine as it roared up the mountain that night in the pouring rain. The recollection of that moment made Lily shudder.

"You okay, Lily?" Steamboat asked.

"I'm fine." Lily replied, "For just a moment, I was remembering something from the night he found me. I'm good. Let's go meet this man and find out what really happened."

They walked through the well-maintained yard to the bright red front door. They rang the doorbell and a tall, well-groomed, middle aged man opened the door. His khaki pants and a freshly pressed button down dress shirt made him look more like a businessman than a truck driver.

Steamboat asked, "Are you Brandon Gates?"

The man paused, looked at them both, and then back at Lily again and studied her face.

"Thank God! I can't tell you what it means to me to know you're okay."

He continued, as Lily and Steamboat glances at one another, "Please forgive me. I know you must have questions. Lord knows the police sure did."

Lily nodded, "I do."

"I knew I ran the risk of being caught lying about where I found you, but I didn't have a choice. I'll explain everything." He stepped back and waved them inside.

Lily wasn't sure what to expect from this man, but this wasn't it.

They walked into the house and sat down in the living room. Lily sat on the brown leather sofa with Steamboat, while Brandon sat in a matching leather recliner next to them.

"Would either of you like a drink or something to eat?" he asked.

Lily responded quickly, "No thank you. I'd rather you explain why you did what you did.

"But first let me say this. I'm not here to get you into any trouble. The police have no idea that I was able to recall what really happened, and I have no intention of telling them, so long as you tell me the truth. Does that sound fair to you?"

Brandon took a deep cleansing breath, paused momentarily, then began to explain. "Agreed. What I'm about to tell you is the truth, but you should know, if you share this information to anyone my life will be in jeopardy."

He placed his hand over his heart. "But since I jeopardized your life to protect mine, I feel it's only fair that I risk it.

"First, you should know that I was a paramedic for a number of years, a long time ago, so I was able to keep you stable enough to make the trip. You were pretty much unconscious for most of the drive, with occasional moments of lucidity. But I was able to control the bleeding until I dropped you off at the hospital.

My hope was the police wouldn't get involved, and that I would never be discovered as the person who dropped you off, but when the detective came knocking on my door, I knew I needed a credible story to avoid getting into trouble."

"I'm recently divorced, and the divorce settlement has left me with little to no money to live on. So, about six months ago, I decided to take up an offer that an acquaintance made to me six years ago.

"I'm basically, in a nutshell, a drug mule. I drive to the mountains of West Virginia once a week and pick up a load of drugs — not important what kind — and I drive them back here to sell. It's not something I'm proud of, but I do it for the money.

"That's why I couldn't stop anywhere after I picked you up. I had to go straight to my drop location first. I had a million dollars worth of illegal drugs in my truck. I wouldn't have even stopped for you if you hadn't been waving."

"You're lucky I didn't run over you completely. We're lucky I was able to hit my brakes in time, that I only tapped you with my truck. Honestly, I can't believe you survived. I knew you needed surgery, that you were in critical shape when I dropped you off at that hospital.

"Like I said, I'm putting my life in your hands with this information."

Lily began to reconcile what she was hearing with her own truth. As she recalled the events of that day, her eyes began to well up with tears. She buried her face into Steamboat's chest and began to cry. He wrapped his arms around her. Lily cried for several minutes, while Steamboat and Brandon sat in silence.

Lily finally gathered herself, and stood and walked over to Brandon's recliner. Brandon got up, and Lily looked him in the eye, paused for a few moments, then hugged him.

"Brandon Gates," Lily softly said, "You saved my life. I will forever be grateful for that. You may not be aware of it, but at the very moment when you put me in your truck, you became an angel and a servant of God. You are not only forgiven, but you will forever be in my prayers.

"Your secret is safe with me, and with my dear friend William. You have my word as a Marine. Isn't that right Steamboat?"

"Yes Sir, my word as a Marine," said Steamboat.

Lily grabbed Steamboat by the hand. "It's time for us to go. We've got a long road ahead of us."

Lily sat up resolutely in her seat as they drove out of the neighborhood.

"Next stop, Bridlewood."

9
WHEN JUDAS, WHO HAD BETRAYED HIM...

F ather Richard woke up at 5:30, as usual, on a cool and crisp Tuesday morning. The first thing he did was recite his favorite prayer, "Hail Mary, full of grace, the Lord is with thee, blessed art thou among women, and blessed is the fruit of thy womb, Jesus. Holy Mary, Mother of God, Pray for us sinners now, and at the hour of our death. Amen."

He added, "And Holy Mary, please intercede on Janet's and my behalf. You know we are in love and very much want to be together, but, as much as I try, there are obstacles in our way that I cannot eliminate on my own. I ask you, Blessed Mother, to pray for me as I work toward the goal of uniting Janet and myself under the glorious eyes of God. Give me the strength I will need to do God's will. Amen." He ended by motioning the sign of the cross.

He got out of bed, walked over to the picture of his late wife, picked it up, and kissed it. "Jan, thank you for coming back to me in the holy vessel of Janet. Be patient, my beloved. The time is near." Richard again made the sign of the cross, and headed into the bathroom to prepare for the day.

He hummed hymns all of the way to church and was surprised to find the door locked when he grabbed the handle. Then he remembered, *Oh yes, Lily won't be here to unlock the church before everyone else arrives, like she's always done.*

Richard smiled as he shook his head and reached into his pocket to get his own keys. He unlocked the door, walked in, and began to prepare the church for the day. It wasn't long before the staff began to arrive and children poured into the school to begin the new day.

At the staff meeting that morning, everyone was asking were Lily was. Cindy was especially curious, and told them, "I've tried calling her several times, but her phone just goes to voicemail. I'm worried that—"

Father Richard interrupted Cindy. "Everyone, Lily is fine. She was feeling a little stressed out, so she requested some time off to head to the mountains for some meditation and prayer. I, of course, agreed."

Cindy, not comforted, said, "But still, I think—"

"I'm sure she's just turned her phone off so as not to be disturbed. Now let's begin with our meeting, please."

After the meeting was over, Father Richard went into his office. The first thing he did was pick up the phone to call Tonya Rodriguez, a member of the church council. She was a wealthy, single woman who was very fond of him. She'd often come to his defense during discussions about former married priests.

They exchanged pleasantries, then Father Richard said, "I was hoping you might do your church, and me, a really big favor. There's a much-loved woman in our church, a mother to three children, who needs some help. I'm aware that you own the apartment complex down the street from the church. So I was hoping you would allow her and her children to move into one of your three bedroom apartments.

"The church will pay her rent, but she'll need to move in quickly once her situation comes to a head. I can't tell you her name at the moment. All I can say is that there's abuse going on within their home now, and I'm counseling her in an attempt to save her. Will you step up for your church, once again, Tonya?"

Without hesitation, Tonya responded, "Of course I will, Father. And please assure this woman, know that she's in my prayers."

"God bless you, Tonya. You're such a gift to us."

"God bless *you*, Father, for all of the good work you do to protect your flock. Let me know when she's ready. Have a blessed day, Father."

Father Richard hung up the phone with a magnanimous smile on his face. He immediately texted Janet and asked her to meet him at the rectory for lunch.

He looked at his watch, then walked out of his office and headed toward the sanctuary. It was almost time to give Mass for the school children, who were already filling the pews with their bright-eyed innocence and whispers.

As noon approached, Father Richard anxiously awaited his lunchtime rendezvous with Janet. While pulling into the garage, he called Janet to confirm her arrival time.

Janet answered, "I'm literally around the corner. Leave the garage door open for me, my beloved."

Richard stood in the garage awaiting her as she drove inside. He closed the garage door behind her, and Janet jumped out of her car into his arms, greeting him with a long, deep kiss. They walked into the kitchen and opened a bottle of wine. Richard had Minestrone soup in the slow cooker, hot and ready to eat. He grabbed some French bread off the counter and put it in the oven to crust up.

He turned to Janet, "Janet, God has spoken to me and revealed the path to our eventual union as one in the eyes of God. Let's set the table, and over lunch I'll explain everything."

Janet smiled. "I love you, Richard."

Richard pointed to the cabinet where the expensive china was kept. "Today I would like us to dine with the fine china. It's a special occasion today. Today is the day we set in motion our life together as one."

Janet felt a great deal of anxiety over this unexplained behavior from Richard.

Janet was re-setting the centerpiece when Richard came in with the soup, bread, and butter. He placed the soup bowls on the plates and the bread into a bread basket.

He put the dish of butter down between their two place settings saying, "This butter was churned by an elderly member of our congregation. She's been making it especially for the priests of our church for forty-five years. It's the most delicious butter I've ever put in my mouth. You're going to love it, Janet."

He slowly and meticulously spread a generous amount on Janet's bread and then hand-fed it to her. Each movement seemed to be choreographed.

Janet tasted the piece of bread and smiled. "Richard, that is exquisite. That butter is one of the richest flavors I have ever put in my mouth."

He agreed with a wink and a smile, "I told you so, darling. Now, let's eat. We have a lot to discuss."

After eating half of their meal, Richard took a deep breath and closed his eyes. "Janet, it's time you understand that Curtis is not the man you believe him to be."

"I don't understand, Richard."

"When he came to see me last night, he made his confession. As long as I've been here, he has never made his confession. I was quite surprised at what he had to say—"

Janet interrupted, "Richard, isn't the confessional supposed to be sacred? Are you about to tell me what Curtis said?"

Richard took Janet by the hand. "Janet, in the eyes of God we are a blessed union, and thus I can share anything with you. You are my muse, and you're a part of me. There is no delineation between the two of us. God has given me special dispensation for full disclosure of my life as a priest for His Church."

Janet looked into Richard's eyes and began to tear up, "Oh Richard, I'm overwhelmed that God Himself has blessed us in such a profound way."

Richard was equally touched by the revelation. "Janet, Curtis has been unfaithful to you many times over the years, and he is *not* remorseful. He actually blamed you for his transgressions. He said you were an inadequate lover who withheld sex on a regular basis. He said you were often so involved with the children and your career that you were not the wife a husband like him deserved.

"I told him that he needed to confess these sins to you and ask for your forgiveness. I'm quite sure he will not do as I've asked, because his selfishness is beyond contempt."

Janet began to tremble as tears welled up in her eyes.

Richard took her by her hands, leaned over to kiss her, and continued, "Janet, you don't deserve to be abused this way. What he's done is paramount to practically beating you until you die. In the eyes of God, he's perpetrated an abomination that's unforgivable. It's time that he suffer the consequences of his transgressions."

Janet felt a wave of shock and confusion pinning her against her seat. She couldn't utter a response.

Richard squeezed her hands, and softly prodded her. "I know what I'm about to propose is going to turn your world upside down, but our love has to be your strength, and I need you to trust in God, for it is He who has guided me to this. Can you do this for us, Janet?"

Janet, who'd felt as if the wind had been knocked out of her, tried to pull herself together with a deep breath. She whispered, "Richard, I trust you, and I trust God to guide us. What is it you need me to do?"

Richard stroked Janet's hair and said, "Janet, you are the strongest woman I have ever known. I know you can do what God has asked."

"I will."

"You will need to accuse him of abandonment and withholding of affection. You will also have to accuse him of mental abuse of you and the children. I've arranged a place for you and the children to live and the church will pay your expenses while you transition into the role of the abused wife."

"Oh, Richard, I don't—"

"This won't be an easy journey for you, or for the children, or for any of us, but you can do this, Janet. God and I have faith in you. I know that in the end we will be together, as God wills."

Janet soaked up the confidence and strength coming from Richard. His words of encouragement seemed like the breath of God, filling her spirit with courage and determination. She sat up straight and said, "Richard, I can do this."

Richard reached up, cupped her face in his hands, and said "That's my angel."

Janet continued, "You should know however, that I'm not very surprised to hear of Curtis' multiple affairs. It just hurts to know with certainty. But I am glad you told me. I needed to know that he's not the man I thought him to be. And you've given me the strength to do just as you say, but how do I go about making this happen? I can't just go home and pack up my and the children's belongings and leave."

Richard lifted Janet's hands and kissed each palm, then assured her, "Janet, you just leave it to me. All you need to do is maintain normalcy, and allow me to facilitate the details of the next few days. I promise that leaving Curtis will be easier than you think.

"Do you trust me? And more importantly, do you trust in God?"

Janet closed her eyes and paused before whispering, "I do, my beloved. I do." When they finished lunch, they cleared the table and cleaned up the kitchen together. When they returned to their respective jobs.

When Father Richard returned to the church, he sat behind the desk in his office and called Curtis. Curtis didn't answer, but Father Richard left him a message, "Curtis, this is Father Richard. Would you please meet me at the church at five today? It's important that you make every effort to be here. I'll explain when you arrive. Thank you and God Bless."

He then headed to the sanctuary to hear confessions for the rest of the afternoon. At 4:45 pm, he finished with the last of the confessions and made his way to the front desk, which happened to be Lily's desk, to await Curtis's arrival. He hadn't heard back so he was anxious as to whether or not Curtis would come. He didn't want to call him again, for fear of seeming too aggressive. He knew Curtis was already on edge from the text message he'd received from Lily.

While waiting, Father Richard began rummaging through the desk. He didn't know what he was looking for, but he thought it was possible that Lily might've left something in her desk that mentioned her discovery of the relationship between him and Janet.

As he was looking through the bottom drawer below Lily's printer, he came across a file folder labeled "F.R." It was at the bottom of the drawer beneath a stack of books and pamphlets. Father Richard opened the folder to find an unfinished letter addressed to the Bishop.

Richard felt a sudden tightness in his throat and chest, and the rage tried to rise from within him. He gripped the letter so tightly, the paper began to crumple.

The letter was incomplete, so Lily had obviously not notified the Bishop as of yet. His rage started to subside, and his grip loosened. He thought to himself, *At least she'll never get the chance to complete this letter. Her vindictive behavior is justification enough for her to no longer walk this earth.*

Father Richard ran the folder and the unfinished letter through the shredder that sat beside Lily's desk. As he watched it slowly chew up the evil document, never to be seen again, in walked Curtis.

"Father Richard," Curtis said as he walked through the door, "I got your message. I'm sorry I didn't get a chance to call you back. The restaurant was crazy today, and we had to prepare for a wedding we're catering this weekend. Is everything okay?"

"Well Curtis," Father Richard said with a solemn tone, "we have an important matter we need to discuss. Would you mind coming up to my office for a moment?"

Father Richard got up from Lily's desk and led Curtis to his office on the second floor. Curtis had never been to Father Richard's office and, as they were walking up the stairs, Curtis admired the many paintings. Most were of various Catholic churches throughout the world, but there were also some Christian icons painted by the school's sixth graders for a yearly class project.

"It's a beautiful thing that you've combined classical church paintings with the children's' icons on the same wall." Curtis further said, "It's a refreshing outlook on life. I'm sure having all these children around you all the time brings back fond memories of your family life, as a husband and parent. Do you miss those times, Father Richard?"

Father Richard abruptly stopped and turned to Curtis. "I miss those times every day. There is not a day that passes that I don't think of my beloved wife, and of our life together with my own children."

He turned and continued to the top of the stairs as he spoke, "But it brings me great joy to see the families I see every day. It's truly a gift from God that I'm a part of this church, and I pray every day that no harm comes to any of my flock."

As they entered his office, Father Richard instructed Curtis, "Have a seat on the couch please." Father Richard made his way to the opposite wall and picked up two glasses of whiskey that he'd already prepared for the two of them. He handed Curtis his and sat down in the chair next to the couch.

"Curtis," Father Richard said, "I'm concerned that you haven't spoken to Janet about your affairs. I realize you aren't doing it any more, and I realize you've come to a place in your life where you're content in your marriage, but what if Janet isn't? Women have an intuition that tells them when their husband has been unfaithful, and I truly believe that if you do not confess your transgressions to Janet, you'll cause more harm than good. I'm telling you this as your priest and as your friend. Go home and tell your wife, and ask her forgiveness."

Curtis took a large drink of his whiskey and before he said anything. He thought to himself, *If you think I'm going to let the man who's fucking my wife give me advice on how to wreck my marriage, then you are sadly mistaken. You can go fuck yourself!*

Curtis then took a breath and calmly said, "Father Richard, you may be right, but as your friend, please allow me to come to my own decision as to how and when I address this with Janet. I promise I will, but I have to find the right time. I hope you understand."

Richard had a response ready for this expected reaction. "As your priest, I must inform you that if you're going to accuse Janet of adultery, as you did this past week, yet you refuse to face her about your own transgressions, I must refuse you any further counsel on the subject.

"I might agree to see you and Janet together for marriage counseling; however, unless you get professional help, I can't do anything more. Your career lends itself to too much temptation. You need to make some changes, Curtis, and you need to make them now. Perhaps you need some in-patient psychiatric care."

Father Richard stood up and straightened his collar. "Go home and think about what I've said here, and I hope, after some contemplation and prayer on your part, you'll still consider me your friend. But remember, I'm your priest first and foremost."

When Curtis stood, Father Richard blessed him with the sign of the cross, saying, "Have a good night Curtis, and may God be with you and bless you." Then he motioned Curtis out and closed the door behind him.

He locked his door, then walked over to the antique buffet. He opened the drawer just beneath the whiskey and removed two bottles of prescription medicine. One was for morphine and the other was for ketamine, both labeled for his late wife.

He removed the caps and tipped each bottle in his hand, so that he could see the contents. One pill from each bottle was cut in half. Richard knew that crushing two whole pills into Curtis's whiskey would've been too much. Richard needed him just slightly incoherent, as if he'd had way too much to drink.

A slight grin crept onto his face as he walked over to Curtis' empty whiskey glass, and he carefully wiped the glass clean with a napkin.

He took both whiskey glasses and the pill bottles downstairs to the church kitchen, and washed them by hand. He emptied the contents of both pill bottles into the sink disposal and turned it on. As the pills were being crushed and washed down, he removed the labels off the bottles and ripped them into pieces. He threw the shredded labels into three different trash cans throughout the church. He separated the lids from the bottles and did the same.

He then returned to the kitchen, retrieved the whiskey glasses, and returned them to the buffet in his office. He turned out the lights to his office and went back downstairs, making his way to the sanctuary. He kneeled before the altar and began to silently pray.

10
WHAT I AM DOING YOU DON'T UNDERSTAND NOW, BUT AFTERWARD YOU WILL...

Not long after leaving the church in a state of confusion, Curtis began to have a sick feeling in his stomach. A warmth rose up his body and into his head. He was feeling slightly numb and dazed, he assumed from the outrageous instructions from Father Richard. As he pulled into his driveway, he thought, *I can't believe I just received a lecture about being a good Christian husband, and about confessing my sins to my wife, from the man who is sleeping with my wife.*

Just then, Janet came to the front door to greet him, saying, "I saw you pull up. How was your day?"

Curtis was barely able to understand what she said. He glared at her and said, "How do you think my day was? My wife is having an affair, and I'm pissed about it! Is that the answer you're looking for?"

"Are you drunk?"

"What? No, not drunk..."

"You're slurring your words, and you seem very agitated. I thought you were past this after speaking with Father Richard."

Janet began to get nervous, and wondered, *Why is Curtis acting this way? He's not right.*

Curtis walked over to the dining room table and almost fell as he tried to sit down. "Father Richard can kiss my ass, and if I see him again, I'm going to knock the shit out of him. How's that for Father Richard's little talk?"

Luckily, the children were across the street at Sally's house playing with her children. Janet grabbed Curtis by the shoulders and looked him dead in the eyes, "Curtis, before you start throwing out unfounded accusations, you need to look in the mirror. If you don't think I know about the affairs you've had in the past, then you're sadly mistaken. I forgave you because we're married, and that's what married people do. They forgive.

I am your wife and I'm telling you right now that if you don't stop behaving this way, you're leaving. You're obviously drunk and don't know what you're saying."

"I know exactly what I"m saying, Janet. You're having an affair with our priest, and I can prove it. Come with me."

Curtis grabbed Janet by the hand and led her to their bedroom, grabbing the walls along the way for balance. He pulled Janet into the closet, opened her jewelry box, and pointed to the single earring. "You see that earring that's just sitting there, all by itself? I bought you those earrings for your birthday. But where's its mate, Janet?"

Janet only stared at him with open mouth.

"I'll tell you where its mate is. Follow me."

He stumbled to his nightstand and opened the little drawer on his valet lying on top of the nightstand. Inside was the matching earring with the ruby in the middle.

"Would you like to know where I found this?" Curtis said holding the single earring up between them.

"I found it under the bed that belongs to your priest. The same bed where you've been fucking him for God knows how long. What an abomination. I can't believe you call yourself a Catholic. In fact, I can't stay in the same house with you anymore. You make me sick. And the two of you can both go to Hell!"

Curtis stumbled to the closet and began haphazardly throwing some clothes into a suitcase.

Janet was dumbfounded by his behavior. She didn't know what to do, so she hurried into the living room to call Richard.

"Richard," she said quietly. "Curtis just came home drunk and started yelling and accusing me of having an affair with you again. He's so angry, and he's packing a bag to leave now. I'm frightened. What should I do?"

Richard quickly responded, "Where are the children?"

"Across the street at Sally's house."

"Good. You need to pack a bag for you and the children and meet me at the church as quickly as you can. Do it now Janet. Now!"

"Okay, Richard. I'll meet you there in thirty minutes."

As Janet hung up the phone, Curtis came in, suitcase in hand. As he walked out the door, he turned and said, "I hope you enjoy rotting in hell, you priest-fucking slut!" He slammed the front door behind him, got into his Jeep, and drove away.

Janet immediately called Sally and explained to her what had just happened. She told her that she'd be over to get the children after she packed their clothes. About twenty minutes later, Janet was walking outside with three packed suitcases. She threw them in the car and met Sally in her front yard.

Sally gave Janet a big hug. "I'm so sorry," Sally said softly. "I can't imagine what's gotten into Curtis. I just don't understand, but I agree that you probably shouldn't stay at home tonight, given Curtis' state of mind. Do you want me to have Bob go look for him?"

"No. I appreciate it, but Curtis needs to deal with this on his own. I just need to make sure the children and I are safe. I'll call you later. Thank you Sally," Janet gave Sally a hug.

As the children got into the car, they asked what was going on and why they were leaving. Janet turned toward them and calmly explained, "Kids, your father is very upset and is acting kind of crazy right now. I'm going to take us on a little hotel adventure for the night while your daddy calms down. It's going to be okay. And Father Richard is going to help us. So please, just don't worry. I promise that everything will be all righte in the morning."

As Janet pulled into the church parking lot, Father Richard was waiting for them. He opened the car door for Janet and greeted the children. "Come on into the church guys, and let's hang out for a bit. Your mother and I need to discuss a few things."

Janet hugged Richard for a little too long, and said, "Thank you, Father Richard."

Once inside, the kids began to play in the commons area while Father Richard and Janet went into his office where Janet explained what had occurred. Richard told her, "It sounds like Curtis has had a psychotic breakdown. I'm going to get a hotel room for you and the kids, at the church's expense, of course. I'll book a suite, so you all can have separate bedrooms. I'll book the hotel for three days, and we'll revisit this in the morning.

"Janet, this begins the process for you to leave Curtis in a legitimate manner. He's the bad guy here, not you. Remember that. And remember I love you. In the meantime, I'll order some pizza and drinks for the kids, and they can have a fun adventure at the hotel."

Richard pulled Janet into an embrace, and Janet began to cry. Richard held her tighter and whispered into her ear, "It's going to be all right Janet, I promise."

Janet allowed Richard's peace and strength to envelop her. She felt as though his energy pulsed through her whenever she was in his arms and she listened to his confident assurances. She quickly regained her composure.

They headed into the commons and Janet cheerfully announced, "Okay kids, we're headed to the hotel for some pizza and fun. Are you ready?"

They loaded up the car, and Father Richard led them downtown to the Hotel Bridlewood, the nicest hotel in the city.

Meanwhile, Curtis had checked into the Comfort Inn about three blocks over, with no idea that his family was so close. He'd dropped his suitcase off in his room and walked back outside and down the street to his favorite bar. Luckily, Jerry Hastings, the bar owner and a good friend, was tending bar that night. It was a slow night, so Curtis was the only person there. Curtis explained everything that had happened to him, and being sympathetic to Curtis' plight, Jerry joined him for a few drinks. They drank until two. By this time, Curtis was so inebriated, he could barely stand so Jerry walked him to his hotel room and eased him down. Curtis quickly passed out.

The next morning was especially hard for Curtis. He woke up with little recollection of what had happened the night before. He could remember meeting with Father Richard and having an argument with Janet, but details were missing. He'd been intoxicated many times in his life, but he'd never had such a gap in his memory. He tried calling Janet, but she didn't answer. He texted her three times, but still no response.

He decided to get up, take a shower and head downstairs to the hotel restaurant for some breakfast. He thought, *Maybe some breakfast and coffee will make me feel better.*

Curtis walked into the restaurant and grabbed a plate and a cup of black coffee. He helped himself to the small breakfast buffet that set out for the guests. As he sat down, his phone vibrated. It was a text message from Janet.

Curtis, I am going to have to ask you to not come back home while I or the kids are present. Your abuse was more than I will allow. You've cheated on me and withheld affection from me, and your neglect of me and the children is more than I can take. I will be filing for divorce as soon as possible. Please text me before you come to the house to gather your belongings so we will not be there. I'm sorry it has come to this, but after last night, you have left me no choice. Please do not try to contact me for a few days, while the children and I try to adjust to our new life without you.

Curtis just sat at the table, perplexed and disturbed. He couldn't believe what he was reading. He stared at his food, thinking, *What in the hell is happening? How could my wife be doing this to me?*

He got up from the table, signed the check, and walked out. He got into his Jeep and headed home. His world was crumbling around him, and it all seemed surreal.

When he pulled into the driveway, he noticed Janet's car was gone. He ran into the house and he searched every room. It looked as though no one had slept there the night before.

He ran across the street to ask Sally if she knew anything. When Curtis approached her front door, Bob opened the door and met him on the porch.

"Curtis," he said, "Janet has already told us everything, and she's retained me as her lawyer, so it would do you well to leave now."

"Did she tell you she was sleeping with Father Richard?" Curtis demanded.

Bob barely acknowledged the question, thinking it was preposterous. "Don't be ridiculous Curtis, you're just making yourself out to be a fool by spreading such an outlandish rumor. Don't say anything else, and leave before I call the authorities." At that, Bob walked back into his house and slammed the door.

Curtis knew immediately that he was being set up by Janet and Father Richard. His thoughts now were focused on how in the world he'd go about proving it.

He headed back to his house trying to figure out what to do next. He then gathered the belongings he thought he might need for the next week or two.

As he drove away, he could feel anger building from the bottom of his gut to the capillaries of his cheeks. The idea of losing his wife and family in such a way was outrageous, but he also knew there was nothing he could do about it right now. His only option was to head back to the hotel to evaluate his circumstances and come up with a plan.

After her text message to Curtis, Janet called Richard. "Okay, I said exactly what you told me to say, and I put it in a text message so there would be a trail of proof. What should I do now?"

"Stay in the hotel today and tonight and, when we're all sure that Curtis isn't going to do anything that would endanger you or the children, we can discuss your going home, or to the apartment I have waiting, if necessary.

"Stay inside the hotel room, order room service, and only answer my calls. I'll contact your office to explain what's happening, and I'll contact the principal of the school as well.

"I'll take care of everything. I'm so proud of your bravery. I love you, Janet."

"I love you too." Janet said. "You are my savior."

"I'll call you later. I have a lot to do in the next little bit."

Janet told the children they were going to stay there for another day or so, explaining that their stay at the hotel, with its many amenities, was one big adventure.

Richard immediately called Ms. Randall, the school principal. "Ms. Randall, would you please gather the Sheffield children's school work for the next couple of days? There's been an incident in the household. Janet won't be available for the next few days, so I'll be taking their assignments to her. And when the children do return to school, it's imperative that Curtis not be allowed to pick the children up from school. Is that understood?"

"Of course." said Ms Randall. "If there's anything else I can do, Father, please don't hesitate to ask. And please tell Janet that she and the children will be in my prayers. God bless you, Father Richard."

Father Richard made a couple more calls. One was to the church council members to inform them that church funds were being used to house and feed Janet and her children, along with an explanation. Another call was to Janet's charity. And finally, he called a meeting of all the church staff to inform them of the situation.

By the time the day was finished, nearly everyone at Our Lady of Damascus Catholic Church had heard Father Richard's version of the events that occurred between Janet and Curtis.

The next morning, Curtis was jogging through downtown, as he did every morning. The only store open was Ollie's Bagels. Ollie was a fixture in Bridlewood. He had been in business for forty years. Every morning, as Curtis ran past Ollie's front window, Ollie would be making bagels for the day. Curtis would always wave to Ollie as he passed and Ollie would wave back, with a glowing smile. However, this morning as Curtis waved, Ollie responded with a scowl and did not wave back. Curtis thought to himself that Ollie must be having a bad morning, but Ollie had never before not waved back with a smile.

When Curtis got back to the hotel room he showered and went downstairs for breakfast. Curtis sat down at a table in the small restaurant awaiting the waitress to take his order. The waitress walked by several times but wouldn't acknowledge him. Curtis finally stopped the waitress and said, "Excuse me miss, but could I please order?"

The waitress looked Curtis straight in the eye and said, "Your wife helped me when no one else would a few years ago, and I refuse to serve you, you piece of shit husband. You can go to hell for all I care!" She then turned and went to the kitchen and began talking to the cook, while pointing and glaring at Curtis.

Curtis was distraught that, in less than twenty-four hours, his character was already being disparaged. He got up from the table and went out and got into his Jeep and drove to the McDonald's drive-thru for breakfast. All the while, Curtis was holding back tears at the idea that his life, as he knew it, was coming to an end.

Around 9:30 am he arrived at his restaurant. As he approached the front door, he noticed that someone had spray-painted on the front door, GO TO HELL ABUSER! Curtis lowered his head, shrugged his shoulders and unlocked the door. He went to the cleaning supply closet and got bleach and a few rags so he could try to remove the graffiti. It took him about an hour, but he was able to remove most of the paint. Curtis soon realized that there was only one person who showed up for work. Three other employees were no shows. He unlocked the doors anyway and awaited his customers. They waited, and waited, and waited. Finally, around 1:30pm he sent his sole employee home and closed up for the day.

Curtis got in his Jeep and decided to drive to the church. He pulled up to the curb in front and just sat there. He watched as a few parishioners walked in and out. A couple noticed Curtis sitting there and gave him a look of hate and disdain. About thirty minutes passed and the flashing lights of a police car caught Curtis's eye in his rear view mirror. He didn't give it much thought until the flashing lights were directly behind him. An officer got out of the patrol car and made his way to Curtis's window. Curtis rolled down his window and recognized the officer as one of his patrons from his restaurant. Curtis asked, "How's it going Pete? I haven't seen you in a few days at the restaurant."

Pete responded,"And you'll never see me there again. Curtis, there was a complaint called in that you are trespassing. I'm going to have to ask you to leave immediately or I will have to take you into custody."

Curtis looked at Pete with a curious bewilderment and said, 'Pete, this is my church. My place of worship. How can I be trespassing?"

Pete repeated himself in a loud voice, "Curtis, I will arrest you if you don't leave immediately. You are not wanted here. Leave, now!"

Curtis rolled his eyes at the officer and then drove away. As he rounded the corner just down from the church, his eyes began to well up with tears. A few moments later, he pulled into a gas station and over to the side of the building and began to weep. He cried out as loud as he could, "God, how could this be happening to me?" He gripped the steering wheel so hard that knuckles turned white and his fingernails were digging into his palms on the other side. He sat there crying for the next ten minutes.

As he finally composed himself, he pulled out of the gas station parking lot and headed for home. As he pulled into his driveway, he realized he was not welcome there either. He stared at the window of his son's bedroom and imagined the horrible things Janet must be telling him about his father. Suddenly Curtis's sorrow turned to anger. He left and headed downtown. He went into the local bar and began to drink. As Jerry served Curtis his first drink, he said, "Enjoy your drink Curtis, and know that there's no judgement here my friend. Let me know if you need anything else." Curtis raised his glass to Jerry and said, "Here's to life as I know it, falling off a cliff and exploding at the bottom of the canyon." Curtis remained there for the remainder of the day and evening, drinking and watching the stream of mind-numbing broadcasts on television that hung behind the bar. Around eleven, he stumbled his way out of the bar and down Main Street toward the hotel. As he arrived at the front door, he paused for a moment and sat down on the bench beside the entrance to the hotel, not wanting to go to his empty room, still grappling with all that had happened.

He dozed off.

The next thing he knew, he was being jerked off of the bench by a harsh grip of a man's hand on his bicep. It was officer Pete.

For a brief moment during his semi-conscious state, Curtis felt relief upon seeing a friend, at the possibility of a friend reaching out. For that brief moment, Pete's hold on him was like water in the desert.

He looked, then lowered his head, saying, "Pete...thank God—"

"All right Curtis," Pete interrupted in a loud, stern voice. "I'm arresting you for being drunk in public. Let's go." Pete handcuffed Curtis and threw him in the back of the police car. He drove four blocks to the police station, took Curtis inside, fingerprinted and booked him. Pete didn't make eye contact with Curtis the entire time. It was as if Pete never knew him prior and treated him like a common criminal. When Pete was finished with the booking process, he took Curtis into a tiny room on the other side of a large door and said, "Take all your clothes off and get into this cell. I'll be back in a little while."

Moments later, Curtis was lying naked in the drunk tank. He sat against the gray wall behind him, clutching his legs because it was so cold. All he could think was how cold it was and he was actually naked. He closed his eyes for a moment, then fell asleep.

Curtis woke up around three, shivering and began calling for someone to come help him.

An officer that Curtis didn't recognize, a gruff and rather rotund man, came to the cell and said, "What do you want, inmate?"

"Why am I naked? I'm freezing. Can I have a blanket?"

"You're in the drunk tank, so you get no clothing or a blanket, but you can have this." The officer reached over beside the cell and grabbed an orange, sleeveless robe that looked more like a thin life jacket, only it felt like cardboard.

Curtis lowered his head and looked across the cell to see three more prisoners, all wearing the same thing. They were curled up in tight balls on the floor, with their so-called robes, trying to sleep. They too, were shivering from the cold concrete floor.

Curtis chose his own spot on the floor and curled up in a ball, trying to cover what parts of his body he could with the stiff prison garment. He began to silently weep, using the collar of the paper garment to keep his eyes dry. He figured this was no time to appear weak, based on only his knowledge of crime TV.

He laid there the rest of the morning, shivering, and *not* sleeping.

As 6am arrived, an officer came by with four paper trays of food. He pushed them through a tray sized slot in the bars and said, "Eat. You've got five minutes." The other three cellmates grabbed their food and began to eat. Curtis looked at the plate containing a stale biscuit, a piece of deli ham and a few burnt pieces of potato.

Curtis looked at the other inmates and said, "I'm not hungry. Do you guys want this?" The younger of the inmates, a highly tattooed man with the grim reaper on the side of his face, said, "Thanks, old man." He grabbed Curtis's tray and shoved the food into his mouth like a starving orphan. Curtis watched a spider web tattoo on the boy's neck pulsate with each swallow.

Exactly five minutes later, the officer returned for the empty trays. Curtis asked, "Officer, when am I getting out of here?"

The officer answered as he walked away, "Someone will be here in a few minutes to discuss your release."

Two more agonizing hours passed. The cold had settled into Curtis' bones, and he fantasized about thawing out his body in front of a large fireplace. Only, he no longer had a fireplace, just a lonely hotel room. His depression grew.

Finally, an officer appeared saying, "Sheffield, come with me." He opened the door, grabbed Curtis by his arm and walked him to a small room.

Inside was a young officer behind a wooden table. He was thin, immaculately groomed, with a thick head of hair. He shoved a paper across the table and said, "Here's a summons to pay a fine for your charge of drunk in public. Here are your clothes and belongings. You can pay the clerk on your way out."

The officer opened the door and directed Curtis to the front desk where Curtis paid the fine. He would've given his last nickel to get out of this hell-hole.

He walked out the front door and down Main Street to the hotel, where he went to his room and took a long, hot and steamy shower. Then he lay in the bed and slept for the rest of the day.

The next few days culminated in the demise of Curtis's reputation as a husband, father and businessman. His restaurant came to a standstill, with no customers and every catering job cancelled for the foreseeable future. By the time Friday rolled around, Curtis had only one employee working and only a handful of customers came into the restaurant, and they were all tourists from out of state.

Every time Curtis would see someone from the church or the community, they would all but turn the other direction, and no one would even look Curtis in the eye.

Curtis decided to temporarily close the business so he could come to grips with what was happening to him and reassess his life.

On Friday, he summoned the courage to text Janet for the first time since she kicked him out of the house. *Janet, I sincerely hope we can open a line of communication for the sake of the children, if nothing else.*

Janet responded, *Yes Curtis, I agree we need to try and get along. Even though you have some major problems, you've always loved your children and been a good father. But until we can reconcile our differences, you'll only be able to see them when I am not at home. I do not want to see you. I have to go to the office to catch up on paperwork on Sunday afternoon, so if you want to visit the kids around 4pm, that would be fine. Sally and Bob will watch them until you get there.* Curtis responded, *Thank you Janet. Tell the kids I love them very much.*

Janet's final text read, *I will, and I'll let them know you will see them Sunday afternoon.*

Curtis had the first smile on his face since he woke up in the hotel room earlier in the week. His only other thought was, *Why is Janet working on Sunday? She's always said she would never, ever work on a Sunday because that was a day for family and church...* He quickly shook it off. After all, he was going to see his children again. That joyous thought gave him a reprieve from his current funk. He just hoped today would be a good day with his children. His thoughts were conflicted between his role as a father and a husband, but he was determined to show his children how much he truly loved them.

11
FOR JEALOUSY MAKES A MAN FURIOUS, AND HE WILL NOT SPARE WHEN HE TAKES REVENGE...

On Saturday afternoon, Curtis was sitting in his hotel room watching college football and drinking a few beers when he heard a knock on the door. He got up and opened the door. Lily was standing before him with a man he had never seen before.

"Lily?" Curtis asked with surprise "What are you doing here?" He stood back, saying, "If you're here to lecture me about my sinful ways, please don't bother."

Lily and Steamboat followed him inside, closing the door behind them.

"I've tried explaining my side of this story for days now, but nobody will listen or believe me. I'm exhausted." He slumped down in a chair at the table, picked up a half-full bottle of beer, and took a swig. "All I want is to be left in peace, to watch football, drink, think about finally being able to see my children...and try to forget about my wife screwing the priest, which no one believes is actually happening. So please don't tell me I'm delusional and that I need to get professional help."

"Curtis," Lily said, "I'm the person who sent you the text message about your wife and Father Richard."

Curtis stared up at Lily, stunned into silence. He shook his head, trying to process this new information. Finally, a tear rolled down Curtis' cheek. He got up, went to Lily, and hugged her tightly.

Lily winced in pain. "Careful Curtis, I've just been in the hospital for emergency surgery, and I'm still very sore."

"What happened? Where have you been all week? Why haven't you come forward to defend me and verify my story to anyone? I don't understand."

Lily raised her hand to calm him, and to explain.

Curtis, running his hands through his hair asked, "Do you realize what I've been through this week?"

"Curtis, sit down, give us a beer, and listen to what I have to tell you," Lily said. Pointing to Steamboat, she said, "Curtis, this is William. He's a dear friend of mine from when I was with the FBI many years ago."

Steamboat shook Curtis' hand. "Everybody calls me Steamboat. Pleasure to meet ya, sir."

Curtis motioned for them to have a seat at the small table and went to pull the rest of his 6-pack out of the fridge. He grabbed the remote and turned off the TV.

"Curtis," Lily said in a calming tone, "What I'm about to tell you will shock you, but please don't interrupt me until I am finished."

Curtis nodded his head in agreement.

"Good. Now listen carefully..."

Lily then explained everything, from the time she suspected something was going on between Father Richard and Janet to their attempted murder of her. She described how Steamboat was able to mend her back to health and back to Bridlewood. She told Curtis about all the evidence she'd collected, but also how Janet and Father Richard had taken it. Then she said something that jolted Curtis straight up in his seat.

"Curtis," Lily said in a soft voice, "Father Richard and Janet don't know I'm still alive. They also don't know that, even though they took my camera and my notebook, I'd saved all the images to the cloud."

Curtis was eager to respond, but, he waited, almost trembling in his seat.

Lily summed up her story with a challenge. "So the question I need to ask you is this: Do you want to walk away from your marriage and your life as you know it, or would you like to handle this *in house*, so-to-speak, with just the three sitting right here at this table? The call is yours to make, Curtis. Which will it be?"

Curtis was dumbfounded and elated at the same time. He took a moment to consider what he'd just heard.

Finally, he said, "Well, Lily, I have a question for you, first. Why haven't you gone to the authorities? After all, he and Janet left you to die on that mountain. Yes, I've lost my wife, my family, and reputation so far. I've also lost my priest and someone I thought was my friend, not to mention my faith, but you could've lost your life. What they did to me was immoral, but what they did to you is a crime. So, what do *you* say, before I decide anything."

Lily leaned back in her chair and with no hesitation said, "Curtis, I'm alive and I'll be fine. I've been through worse in my life, but what this so-called priest has done strikes me at my spiritual core. It would bring me a greater satisfaction to see him defrocked and publicly disgraced than anything the legal system could do to him. Plus, allowing the authorities to handle it would potentially send your wife, the mother of your children, to prison as well. So I'll be just fine with whatever decision you make."

Curtis only needed to think for a few seconds before agreeing, "I say we let Janet and Father Richard decide what they want. I'm pretty sure they'll be together tomorrow, because Janet's invited me to visit with the children around four tomorrow afternoon while she works at her office. I say the three of us pay them a little visit during their rendezvous and let the two of them decide their own fate. What do you think, Lily?"

"I think we're on the same page." Lily nodded and smiled as they all three raised their beer for a toast. "It's time we take back our lives, and our church. Amen, I say. Amen."
, putting together ideas they hoped would expose the truth, once and for all.

And so, on Sunday, there was Curtis, acting as an amateur detective in order to carry out their plans. This is how he found himself crouched beneath the kitchen window of the rectory after having witnessed his wife kissing his priest.

As Curtis sat there, his phone began to vibrate. It was Lily. He slowly got up, walked away from the house, and answered, "I just saw them kiss and head toward the bedroom. Wait for me on the back patio and I'll signal you when it's time."

Curtis waited around for a moment and then made his way to the front of the house. As he walked past the bedroom window, he could clearly hear moans coming from Janet.

Curtis shook his head, as though removing fresh snow, gathered himself and continued to the front door.

He pulled out the key Lily had given him to the front door of the rectory. Most every staff member had a copy, just in case someone was needed inside the rectory when the priest wasn't available.

Curtis, very slowly and quietly, placed the key into the lock. He froze for a second. He felt as if he were stepping into the lions' den, but he found the necessary determination. It wasn't so much through a prayer, but in the knowledge and recollection of being on the right side of the moral fence with righteous friends lifting him up.

He turned the key gently. Once unlocked, then the handle with the same care, and quietly opened the door. As he walked into the foyer, he turned and gently closed the door.

As he went toward the hallway, he could hear them moaning in ecstasy. Curtis felt like someone was punching him in the stomach, but he knew what had to be done.

He then walked past the bedroom door, which was closed, and continued to the other end of the house to the back door, which led to the patio. He slowly opened the door and waved his hand. Lily and Steamboat quickly and quietly entered. They stealthily made their way to the dining room table.

In complete silence, Lily pulled a laptop computer out of her bag and began to type. Steamboat stood behind her, with a 9mm Glock in his hand, as if he were guarding the President himself.

Curtis noticed Father Richard's and Janet's cell phones on the kitchen counter, so he grabbed the phones and handed them to Steamboat. Then he went to the liquor cabinet and quietly retrieved the unopened bottle of thirty year old Scotch that had been given to Father Richard by none other than the Pope, himself, to commemorate Richard's induction as a priest. Father Richard was proud of it and had spoken of it several times.

Curtis opened it.

Then he laid out five glasses on the dining room table, with the open bottle of Scotch beside them.

Lily gave the nod that she was ready.

Curtis took a deep breath.

He started down the hallway toward the bedroom.

He could hear Father Richard and Janet making pillow talk as he inched his way closer to the bedroom door. He froze in place to steady himself for the task ahead.

He could hear the two of them saying "I love you" over and over, then finally, Curtis took one last cleansing breath, lowered his head and closed his eyes, as if to say a prayer. He raised his head, opened his eyes, and with his right hand, he clasped the door knob and turned it.

In one swift move, he walked in to catch the dumbstruck lovers in their embrace. Before they could react, Curtis went up to the side of the bed, with his cell phone held out and recording. "Good afternoon Father Richard, and Janet. Would you please join me in the dining room? We have a few matters to discuss."

Janet and Father Richard's eyes zeroed in on Curtis' phone, knowing that they were being recorded. Father Richard's jaw clenched, his dark eyes fixed on Curtis. With one hand, Janet grabbed the sheet and pulled it up to cover herself, and with the other, she clutched Richard's bare arm.

Curtis waited. He felt as though he were outside of himself, watching this go down. And he was thankful for it. If he allowed his emotions to get swept up, he wouldn't be able to continue their plan.

Father Richard nodded to Janet and patted her hand, as if she couldn't make a move without his permission. Janet reached down with trembling hands to get her clothes, and then hurried to the bathroom.

Father Richard got out of bed and began to dress, slowly and deliberately. He didn't utter a word, but he never took his eyes off Curtis.

Finally, as Janet emerged fully clothed from the bathroom, Richard stepped toward Curtis, pointed a finger in his face, and threatened, "I don't know how you got in here, but we will be calling the police and you will be arrested for breaking and entering. And I may be sixty-five years old, but I'll be taking that phone away from you, and you'll pay for invading my home."

Curtis smiled, "That's big talk coming from the man who's fucking my wife. You haven't begun to see my anger, old man. Now I'd like the two of you to make your way to the dining room, please."

The lovers began their walk down the long hallway, hand in hand.

As they neared the dining room, Curtis turned off the camera to his phone. When Janet and Richard rounded the corner to the dining room, there sat Lily, behind her computer screen. Steamboat stood behind her with his arms crossed. Steamboat's fun was visible.

Lily looked them both in the eyes the moment they stepped into the room, "Father Richard, Janet...It's so good to see you both. How have you been?"

Stunned Richard and Janet sat down beside one another on one side of the table, opposite Lily. Richard stroked Janet's forearm, trying to comfort her. Her eyes were closed, as if she was trying to be somewhere else in her own mind. As Richard stroked her forearm he said, "It's going to be okay my love. Try to relax." Janet slowly opened her eyes and regained her composure. Richard looked her in the eye and smiled.

"Where are my manners?" exclaimed Curtis. "Let me offer the two of you a drink. I figured since this was such a special occasion, we should have something special. Father Richard, I took the liberty of opening the Pope's personal gift to you so that we could all celebrate the wonderful life upon which you and Janet are about to embark. True love is a beautiful gift from God, as such, it should be celebrated with friends. Don't you think?"

Curtis and Lily saw the rage building in Father Richards face and in his eyes, and the utter fear frozen in the eyes of Janet. Father Richard clinches his jaws tightly as Curtis poured five double shots of Scotch. He placed the glasses side by side as he poured and never lifted the bottle between each glass, as the whiskey spilled onto the dining room table between the glasses. He then placed a glass in front of both Janet and Richard, and handed the others to Lily and Steamboat.

"Let's drink a toast," Curtis proclaimed. "To Richard and... You don't mind if I call you Richard do you? After all, you're not going to be a priest for much longer. To Richard and Janet. May their love bring them great happiness and strength, because the next few days are going to certainly test that love, I'm sure."

Curtis, Lily, and Steamboat all took a sip.

Curtis said, "I do believe that's the best whiskey I've ever had in my mouth for as long as I've been alive. *It's exquisite.* Our Pope sure knows his Scotch. Do you think I could convince him to give me a bottle, Richard?"

He pushed a glass forward, saying, "Richard, you must try this Scotch. So smooth and complex."

Neither Richard nor Janet responded.

"Oh well," Curtis shrugged, "You have no idea what you're missing. I guess we should get down to business now." He nodded toward Lily. "Lily, this is your show now. Show 'em what you got, my friend."

Lily took a good hard look at each of them and said, "The two of you left me for dead on that mountain. Despicable. If it weren't for the kindness of strangers and the grace of God, I wouldn't be here today to show you that the love the two of you think you share is truly blind." Lily turned the laptop around so Richard and Janet could see the screen, and then Lily hit the return key.

"As you will plainly see," Lily stated, "The slideshow you're watching is a record of you two coming and going from the rectory, your sacrilegious communion and sex on the mountaintop."

Lily and Richard stared at the screen as their misdeeds flashed before them.

"Curtis has filled me in on what's occurred over the past week as well. Curtis and I have decided not to pursue criminal charges for what you did to me. However, we are going to ask a few things of you in return for this act of kindness."

Father Richard tilted his head. "Oh?"

"First, Curtis gets to move back into his home, with his children.

Janet, you'll explain to all your friends and fellow parishioners that you simply overreacted and made a mistake by asking for a divorce. Can you do this?"

Janet pursed her lips together, and silently nodded.

"Secondly, Richard, you'll go back to work tomorrow, on your day off, and work for the rest of the week as normal. You'll prepare a Homily for Sunday's Mass explaining how you and Janet have fallen in love and how the two of you tried to destroy Curtis's reputation for the sole benefit of your relationship."

Richard's eyes narrowed, as a crimson anger rose to his face.

"You'll explain that you're leaving the priesthood so that the two of you can live your lives together. When you're finished with your Homily, you'll walk down from the altar, take Janet by the hand, and the two of you will leave the church and never return. Curtis and his children will not be at Mass, so as to prevent traumatizing them. Is that clear, Richard?"

Richard silently nodded, his face was twisted with pent-up rage.

Lily shut the computer screen and put the computer in her purse, "I believe our business is concluded here. Curtis will return home now and my colleague and I will head back to my house for rest. You two can stay here and contemplate how this next week will unfold for you. But don't forget, we're literally holding your combined fates in our hands, and we've decided to show you the mercy that you were not willing to show either of us. I pray you will receive this gift with humility and grace."

Lily grabbed the remainder of the Scotch, and poured Steamboat, Curtis, and herself one last drink. They then they walked out the front door with Steamboat guarding their rear.

As the front door shut behind them, Richard grabbed Janet's still trembling hand and said, "This is not over. God has a plan that does not bow to the sin of blackmail. We're blessed by God, and he'll continue to guide us in defeating these angels of Satan. Janet, do you trust in God and me to see us through this tribulation?"

Janet finally felt like she could breathe again when she felt Richard's powerful confidence fill the room. She took a deep, shaky breath, and said. "Yes, Richard. You're the most important person in this world to me. Please make this okay."

Richard held her close, stroking her lavender scented hair. He kissed her and said, "Janet, I promise you, as a servant of God Himself and of all that is good and holy, I will make this right. God will not forsake us, I promise."

12
IN HIM, WE HAVE REDEMPTION THROUGH HIS BLOOD...

Curtis, Lily and Steamboat left the rectory, but at Lily's insistence, they headed straight for Curtis's restaurant. She had told Curtis that there was something important she needed to discuss with him, and it couldn't wait. As they were drinking freshly brewed coffee, Cindy walked in. Lily got up from her chair and rushed to greet her with a hug.

Cindy, with tears welling up in her eyes, said, "Lily, I'm so glad you called me. I knew something was wrong. I knew Father Richard was lying about where you were, but I couldn't figure out how or why. The kids at church have all been asking about you, and I didn't know what to say. All the kids love you so much. I just said you were on vacation.

"I also knew that Father was having an affair with Janet, but I just couldn't bring myself to believe it. I met him at the rectory the other week and I heard Janet's voice in his bedroom. He just ignored it and rushed me out of the house. It was all very creepy."

She kept shaking her head in disbelief, then turned to Curtis open-armed, motioning for him to give her a hug. "I'm so sorry this has happened to you, Curtis. The things Father said really painted you as a horrible person. It was all so confusing, especially knowing that the two of you were friends. I can't believe this is happening."

"Thank you, Cindy. The past few weeks have definitely been the worst of my life, but it's good to know that it will all be coming to an end soon."

Lily introduced Steamboat to Cindy, and they all sat back down at the table. Lily turned to Cindy, handed her two flash drives and then handed Curtis two flash drives. She instructed them, "Cindy, Curtis, these flash drives contain exact copies of all the evidence that incriminates Father

Richard and Janet. You'll each need to keep them in safe locations. This is very important. Can you both do this?"

Cindy and Curtis both nodded, then Cindy asked, "Lily, I understand, and of course, I'll gladly do as you ask, but why are you being so cloak and dagger about this? We need to get Father Richard out of our church and out of our lives."

Lily replied, "Because I won't be here. What neither of you know is that Father Richard has familial ties to a certain powerful family organization out of New York.

"As you both know, I used to be an analyst and field agent for the FBI, and I helped track down organized crime in the Northeast. When Father Richard was first assigned to our Parish, I'd made a few inquiries about him, because I'd recognized his last name from my work in the FBI. He's the only member of his family who didn't appear to take part in the family business. He was an attorney, and from time to time he represented the family in various ways. He helped with IRS problems and legal documentation for a lot of the family's legitimate businesses. We believe that he wasn't completely removed from their business, but since he was a Deacon for the Catholic Church, he gained legitimacy and credibility. While I was in South Carolina with Steamboat, I reached out to a couple of my contacts in New York."

Lily teared up as she reached out to hold Curtis' and Cindy's hands. "My truck, and any evidence of the accident are gone. The wreck has effectively been deleted from history. I only have my word about it. The problem is, I can't use just my word in a court of law without physical evidence of a crime and it would put the two of you at risk."

She said to Cindy, "I'm sorry to have involved you, but you're my dearest friend, and I couldn't leave this with Curtis alone. I trust you. The good news is that Father has no idea you're involved. So let's keep it that way."

Cindy nodded. Curtis has been staring down at the floor but he too, apologized to Cindy. "I'm sorry you got swept up into this. I'm sorry that all of us have to deal with this..."

Lily looked at Curtis, gave his hand a squeeze, and said, "We're all in this together, as it should be. But, I must tell you that I was informed, just as I left the rectory, that Father has already made a call to his family.

"So we have to act quickly. I've no doubt that one or more persons in the family are on their way here as we speak. Curtis, you're going to go home, as we stated. Tomorrow morning, you're going to call Father

Richard and tell him you've had a slight change of heart. Tell him you and I have discussed the situation, and you've decided the humiliation to your family, and especially your children, has caused you to reconsider his public declaration at next Sunday's Mass. You'll instead ask him to step down quietly and take Janet away from this town. But tell him you want joint custody of the children—"

"Wait a minute Lily. Then what was that whole theatrical show at the rectory about?"

Lily laid her hand on Curtis' arm and sighed. "That was for you Curtis. And a little bit for me as well. That son-of-a-bitch needed to be knocked down a peg or two, and we both deserved to look him in the eye just as we did.

"But the reality is that his ties to his New York family are more than we can fight without great harm befalling us. But hopefully his real enemy is me now, not you. He's already won the prize: your wife. Now he has to find a way to exit the church. I don't believe he would harm you or the children because it would irreparably harm his relationship with Janet. And his relationship with Janet is all he has now. His priesthood is over, so he won't risk losing Janet."

Steamboat, who'd remained silent added, "I'll be leaving with Lily from here, so your only communication will be through this email." He handed Cindy and Curtis each a piece of paper with an email address on it.

He pointed firmly at the papers they held, and instructed them. "I would suggest that you memorize the email address in case you lose these pieces of paper, because you won't be able to reach Lily otherwise...unless she contacts you.

"Her phone number will change from time to time, so if you do see a number on your phone that you don't recognize, there's a good chance it's Lily."

Cindy reached for Lily's hand, which unlike her own, was steady and sure. Lily's strength and integrity radiated from her, comforting them all. It was no wonder so many people loved her, trusted her, and depended on her.

Curtis said, "I feel like God has turned his back on me. How could this be happening to all of us?" Lily calmed him.

Lily smiled. "Curtis, you'd be surprised how many things like this happen every day around the world. It's unfortunate for all of us involved, but it's important we don't lose hope, or our faith in God. Something like this can rock your faith, but don't let it. God is real, and he's with all of us. Don't forget that."

Then they sat in silence for a few minutes, obviously contemplating the immensely strange, and potentially dangerous situation in which they had all found themselves. The only sound was the traffic outside the restaurant.

Curtis was the first to speak, placing his hands flat on the table in front of him. "Okay, then. I believe it may be time to part ways, don't you think, Lily?"

Lily nodded.

Curtis stood up, and straightened his jacket. "Plus I should probably get home to the children. Our neighbor, Sally is watching them at her house right now. And I don't even know if Janet's coming home or not. I'm not sure what to tell the kids. It's going to be an interesting night at my house for sure."

Everyone got up, shared hugs, and went their separate ways.

As Curtis pulled into the driveway of his house, he went straight across the street, retrieved his children, and returned home.

He sat the kids down on the couch and said, "Kids, I'm back home now, and I'm not sure if mommy will be home tonight or not, but I promise you, everything's going to be okay." He rubbed his hands together and asked, "How about I pop some popcorn and we watch a movie together?" The kids seemed anxious and confused, but they were happy and eager to spend time with him. They all agreed to the movie.

When the movie ended, Curtis got them into their pajamas, their teeth brushed and tucked all three children into bed. He could see a little confusion in each of their faces, and it broke his heart, but there was nothing else he could do or say to ease their minds.

Most of his thoughts were now about what was going to happen next. Everything was uncertain and confusing to him, too.

As Curtis was cleaning up popcorn from the couch, he noticed headlights turning into his driveway. It wasn't his wife's Mercedes, but rather, Father Richard's old Volvo. And he wasn't alone. He was accompanied by a tall, slender man in a dark suit. Curtis's heart jumped into his throat.

He spoke out loud, "Stay calm, Curtis. We don't want to alarm the kids, and Richard's not going to harm you or the children."

Curtis quickly ran to his bedroom to grab the pistol out of the small biometric gun safe from the top of his closet, and tucked it in the back of his pants.

At the front door Richard reached up and softly knocked.

Curtis slowly unlocked and opened the door.

13
IF YOUR BROTHER SINS AGAINST YOU, GO AND TELL HIM HIS FAULT...

"I'm here to renegotiate your terms, in a civilized manner. Are you up for it?" Richard asked.

"Of course," Curtis answered. "For the sake of the children, I'm all for whatever keeps the peace,."

"Very good." Richard nodded slowly, with a smile and a wink. "With that being said, I'd like to introduce you to my brother, Anthony Puglisi. He's here to give me moral support and make sure we don't lose our temper. I understand why you did what you did this afternoon and, in fact, I respect the fortitude it took to do it. Nevertheless, there was a lack of mutual discussion and compromise, so let's hash this out, right here and now."

Curtis led the two men to the dining room table and motioned for them to sit down. Father Richard grabbed the seat at the head of the table, and Curtis and Anthony sat on either side of him. Anthony's presence reminded him of the way Steamboat watched over Lily as they'd confronted Richard earlier that evening.

Curtis could feel the sweat forming on his temples and his hands were clammy. A cold shiver suddenly traveled down his spine, because he knew, from the conversation with Lily earlier, that this Anthony character was not here to "keep the peace." He was here to enforce Father Richard's wishes, at all costs.

Curtis summoned up his courage and said, "Could I get either of you a drink?"

"No thanks, Curtis, Let's just get down to business." With narrowed eyes and a slightly twisted grin, he added, "I've had my fill of drinks tonight."

The reference to the bottle of Scotch did not escape Curtis. "I understand that. Very well, what is it you'd like to discuss, Richard?"

Richard first glanced at his brother, nodded his head, turned to Curtis and said. "Curtis, I know Janet and I have hurt you deeply, so I understand your rage and your need for revenge and restitution, but there's another way to move forward, that I believe will satisfy us all."

"I'm listening," Curtis said.

"Good. I am in love with your wife, and your wife is in love with me. However, there are two major obstacles in our way. You and the Church. These obstacles must be removed."

"The simple answer is this. I leave the priesthood and you and Janet get a divorce." He flipped his open palm up and out toward Curtis as if he were offering him a gift. "My proposal is this: You and Janet file for divorce tomorrow morning, and, as your priest, I'll support the decision. After a suitable time, say two months, Janet and I will announce that we've fallen in love, and I will ask permission to be laicized, so that Janet and I can be married."

Curtis recognized that this was *not*, as Richard had suggested, merely a proposal. This was a command, dictated from the high seat of Father Richard, with the weight of his family behind it.

"Curtis, I can give her a glorious life. I may be a priest now, but I haven't always been, as you well know. When I served the Church as a Deacon, I was also a very successful attorney. Very few people know this about me. It was easy to conceal this from public knowledge here, because my one and only client was my family, with its vast financial holdings and businesses.

"My brother, Anthony here," Richard said while giving Anthony a pat on the back, "is the CEO of our family owned business. He's always made sure I didn't want for money, but my calling to the Catholic Church also taught me that money isn't everything. However, I can assure you Janet will want for nothing. I have plenty of love and money to give her.

"And don't worry about the children. You'll always be their father, and I promise I will help raise them with you and Janet as if they were my own children. You can live with that, right Curtis?"

Curtis felt a blistering anger bubbling up inside him at the mere idea of this manipulative, evil human being helping to raise his children, but Curtis also knew he was at a substantial disadvantage here. He was backed into a corner of the lion's den, with no escape and no weapons to defend himself against the powerful beast in front of him.

Tamping down his anger all he could, Curtis turned to Anthony, partly because he couldn't stand to look at Richard anymore. "Anthony, first I want to welcome you to my home, and I appreciate that you're here to support your brother. But, since we're all gentlemen at this table, I'd like to ask you a question, and get an honest response. Is that acceptable?"

Anthony was taken aback, but responded in kind, saying, "Thank you Curtis, and yes I give you my word that I'll be honest."

"Thank you," Curtis said. "What do think about the decision your brother, the priest, has made in regards to leaving the Catholic Church and marrying my wife?"

Anthony leaned back in his chair, stroked his cleanly shaven face and said, "Honestly, I support my brother's decision. I feel he will have a long way to go when it comes to reconciling this decision with the Catholic Church and those who gave him the honor and respect that comes with being a priest, but he's my brother. And I know his heart. If he feels this strongly about Janet, then I will support him any way I can.

"I knew My brother's first wife. I was proud to call her my sister-in-law and my dear friend. If Janet is half the woman my brother has described to me, then she will be welcomed into our family with open arms.

"That being said, I'm sorry you're losing your wife of so many years, and that your family is splitting, but, you know—" Anthony smiled, tilted his head, and gestured flippantly with both hands," sometimes these things happen.

"You showed some balls today, also the lengths you'll go to for the love of your family. I can respect that. So can Richard. But now, just try to move on with your life."

Anthony's threat wasn't delivered with the same finesse as Richard's.

"I do think perhaps you should be given...well, certain concessions. But, make no mistake, I'm here for him, not you." Anthony nodded toward Richard. "My big brother, Richard, has always gotten what he's wanted and I'll always support him. I'm sure you can understand that, Curtis?"

Curtis quickly answered, "Of course, I understand that clearly."

Curtis looked toward Richard. "Richard, I have one request. I would like my reputation back, please. You and Janet have effectively destroyed me in the eyes of the Church, the town, and my friends, but I sincerely hope you and Janet have not destroyed me in the eyes of my own children—"

Richard interjected, "Janet and I have not said anything to your children that would in any way damage your standing as their father. I give you my word."

Curtis thought to himself, *You couldn't even keep your word to God, himself. Your word is worthless to me, you bastard!* But instead of saying that, Curtis said, "Thank you, Richard. For that, I'm very truly grateful. But I'm not sure how you plan to repair the damage the two of you've done to me."

Richard took a deep breath, and said, "I'm not sure we can repair all the damage, but maybe we can repair some of it. I'm sure I can convince Janet to walk back some of the things she said about you and I'll see to it that the Church does not condemn you harshly. But Curtis, you have to understand, the night you left my office and went home, you were very cruel to Janet, and I'm not sure if she will *ever* forgive you for that."

Curtis rubbed his temples and shook his head, "I swear, I have no recollection of the things I said to her that night, and I can't even remember how or why I acted that way. I didn't even really drink a lot that night. I just had a beer at work and that one drink of whiskey in your office—"

Richard briefly raised an eyebrow, but he just stared at Curtis, with hands clasped in front of him on the table.

Curtis saw Richard's fleeting micro-expression, and paused. He lowered his head, recalling how his memory loss came shortly after leaving Richard's office. He suddenly realized, *That son-of-a-bitch drugged me. He antagonized me, drugged me, and sent me home, knowing that I would blow up at Janet. What kind of man does that? What the fuck am I going to do?*

Curtis quickly looked up and returned to the conversation, hoping his growing anger wasn't evident. "—but I'm willing to take responsibility for that night. So, if Janet is willing to walk back her harsh statements about me and eat crow, as they say, then I'm sure we can come to an agreement here tonight. I'll move out of the house, and the hotel, and get a place of my own. But I would like an agreement that Janet and I will have joint custody of the children. Do you have a problem with that, Richard.?"

"Of course not, and I insist on helping you with your moving expenses, and with the loss of business you've incurred as a result of all of this." Richard turned to Anthony and nodded.

Anthony reached into his inside suit pocket and pulled out a check for fifty-thousand dollars and handed it to Curtis, saying, "This is from our family to yours. It's a gift. Accept it as such, and not another word will be spoken of it."

Curtis took the check and placed it in front of him on the table, wondering, *How in the hell can you two live with yourselves, trying to buy another man's wife as if you're doing me a favor?* But he only nodded and said, "Thank you, I appreciate and accept your gift."

At that, Richard and Anthony stood up from the table, and Richard said, "Janet is staying at the rectory tonight. When I get back there, I'll explain to her what we've accomplished here tonight. Tomorrow morning,

I'll send her back here to her children, and after you both drop the kids off at school and you've packed your things, you can discuss the details of how to proceed with our arrangement."

Curtis stood up just as Richard and Anthony reached out to shake hands as if they were concluding a business deal.

Curtis nearly choked on his own parting words. "Thank you for your willingness to negotiate, and for not retaliating against my actions earlier today at the rectory."

Richard smiled magnanimously, firmly pumped Curtis's hand, and said, "Think nothing more about it. It's forgotten."

Curtis walked the two men to the front door. As they walked out to the driveway, Curtis closed the door, turned his back to the door and slowly shrunk down until he was sitting with his knees in his chest. He ran both hands slowly through his hair while taking a deep breath and then softly released a breath through his lips, as if blowing out a candle.

His couldn't imagine what his next move would be, or if he even had a move left to play. He sat for a while staring at the floor, until, feeling hopeless, he began to weep quietly into his hands.

Meanwhile, Father Richard found Janet in the rectory sitting on the couch, drinking a glass of Chardonnay.

"This must be your brother, Anthony?" asked Janet, as she got up to meet him.

"Yes, this is my devoted brother, Anthony." Then he pulled Janet toward him to show her off. "Anthony, this is Janet, my reason for living."

As Janet greeted Anthony with a hug, Richard explained, "This man has been my best friend from the time he was born. I looked after him for most of our lives, and now he's here to look after us."

They all went to the living room and Richard laid out the arrangements. "It's important you understand that the next few days will be crucial to the preservation of our reputations and to the path our future holds. You'll stay here tonight, and early tomorrow morning you'll go home to take your children to school and resume your life. Curtis will be moving out tomorrow and we're going to have a less theatrical ending to this situation. The only thing I ask of you is that you not engage in conversation with Curtis in any way.

"I'll accompany you to your house in the morning, and together, we'll take the children to school. Everyone knows I'm acting as your advocate during this rough spot in your marriage, so it won't seem inappropriate at all.

"We'll need to be careful, however, to ensure the timing leads people to believe that our relationship began *after* your separation and divorce from Curtis. Can you do this, Janet?"

"Of course I can. I love you with everything I am, and I trust you with my life. You tell me what to do, and I will do it. Wherever you go, I go. I just want us to be together, and I want the whole world to know it as soon as possible. I hate keeping it a secret from everyone, especially my closest friends."

Richard reached for Janet's hand and took it into his, saying, "Janet, I promise everything will be perfect. Trust me. Would you mind getting Anthony a glass of whiskey? I'm going to show him to the guest room so he can freshen up."

"Of course, sweetheart," Janet said as she made her way to the kitchen.

As Richard showed his brother to the guest room, he whispered, "Have you found Lily and her friend?"

"Not yet, but the boys are working as hard as they can to locate her We should know something by morning. And we've erased all evidence of the accident as well, just as you asked, Richard. It never happened. Don't worry. Everything will go as planned."

"I certainly hope so. "I love this woman, but this needs to be resolved as soon as possible. Please Anthony, make it happen."

As Anthony walked into the bedroom, he turned to Richard, saying, "I will big brother, I will. No worries. You just be sure that this woman is worth the sacrifices you are making. She must be some kind of woman to make you go to such lengths for her."

14
THOSE WHO DO NOT CONFESS THAT JESUS CHRIST HAS COME IN THE FLESH...

The sun was still hiding at five o'clock on this cool Monday morning. Curtis usually woke early to get a run in before the hustle and bustle of family life began. Normally, he enjoyed the stillness and solitude he found in the early hours of the morning, but he mourned the loss of upcoming routines. And he regretted that he might have taken those moments for granted while he had them.

This morning in the quiet darkness Curtis struggled to get moving. He hadn't gotten much sleep but knew he had to get ready for the day.

He got in the shower and let the hot water flow over him for longer than usual, massaging some tension out of his achy muscles. His mind was racing too much lately, and he felt a heavy burden. His business kept him busy and sometimes stressed, but it was nothing compared to the agony of these past few weeks. As the thoughts flooded his mind, he began to cry. He allowed his tears to be washed away until there was no more hot water and no more tears.

He turned the water off and shivered as the cool air hit him. It was an involuntary movement, but perhaps necessary to complete the remainder of his emotional cleansing.

As he was drying himself off, he heard the front door open and shut. He knew it had to be Janet. So he quickly dried his hair with the towel and threw his robe on to head for the front of the house.

He stopped in his tracks when saw Janet and Richard both busy in the kitchen making coffee. Curtis was startled by Richard's presence, but not surprised. He, however, had no desire to rush into another encounter with either of them. They hadn't noticed him yet, so Curtis turned and went back to the bedroom to get dressed.

After he got dressed, he grabbed a suitcase out of the closet and packed a few more clothes. He went into each of his children's bedrooms and kissed and hugged them, telling them that he would see them very soon. He told them their mother and Father Richard were going to be taking them to school, and everything would be just fine.

Curtis walked into the living room to find Richard and Janet drinking coffee and watching the morning news, as if they were a happily married couple already. As if Curtis' departure was predestined. Richard was sitting in Curtis's recliner and Janet was on the couch.

It was maddening to see how Richard was just sliding right into the empty space that Curtis's exile was creating. The thoughts that came to his mind were begging to spew forth onto them, but he knew he had to leave the house without incident. He didn't want to upset the children or fracture the so-called gentlemen's agreement that had been struck the night before.

So, Curtis only smiled as he walked past the couple and said, "Janet, I'll contact you later about getting the rest of my things, and we can make arrangements for filing for divorce and visitation with the children. Does that sound okay to you?"

"Yes, Curtis, that's fine." Janet placed her hands on her chest in an ironic gesture of gratitude and understanding. It's as if the whole exchange seemed to afford her another opportunity to step into sainthood. "And thank you for being so understanding. We can make this work for the children and everything will be just fine."

Curtis swallowed the disgust that was stuck in his throat and walked out the front door without a word. He got into his Jeep and drove away.

Janet woke the children for school. They were groggy and difficult to wake. Eventually, Father Richard poked his head into the rooms, with an authoritative, "Chop-chop, let's get moving." They reluctantly rose and got dressed. When they entered the kitchen, Father Richard was making eggs and toast. They put their book bags down at the door, and plopped down at the table while Janet set out plates in front of them.

Cassandra moved the eggs around on her plate with her fork, and asked, "When's Daddy coming back home?"

Janet walked over to Cassandra, smoothed her hair with both hands, and leaned down to kiss the top of her head. "Don't worry, Honey, you'll see him soon."

Richard tried to distract them with a joke. "Why did the chicken family cross the road?" When no one answered, he smiled broadly and said,

"They thought it was an *egg*-cellent idea." The children looked up and smiled, but just finished their breakfast in silence as Janet focused on cleaning up the kitchen. Janet and Richard then drove them to school, giving them each a hug and a "Love you."

Richard drove back to the rectory where he dropped Janet off at her car in the garage and they kissed goodbye, just like any ordinary couple would. Then, they both went to work. Father Richard went to the church with plans to tackle the day's agenda, just as he did every day.

Janet, however, wasn't going to her office right away, not until she made a slight detour which landed her in the parking lot of a doctor's office.

Dr. Christopher Lennox was married to her best friend, Amy whom she'd texted before leaving the house. She'd asked Amy and Chris both to meet her at his office as soon as possible. His office didn't open until 9:30, but she wanted to see them before the office opened.

Janet sat in her car, waiting only a few minutes before Amy and her husband drove up. Amy got out of her car, went over to Janet, and hugged her.

"What's wrong Janet? Your text sounded so urgent. Has Curtis hurt you?"

Janet grabbed both of Amy's hands and said, "I'm okay, and it's nothing like that, but I do need to see you and Chris in the office, in private."

Chris unlocked the door, and they all stepped inside. Janet took a second to appreciate the tasteful yet minimally decorated front rooms. The simplicity comforted her as they made their way to Chris's office.

Janet shut the door behind them. Chris sat down behind his desk and Amy sat next to Janet in front of the desk. Amy grabbed Janet's hand and held it tight.

Chris said, "Why did you need to see us here, at my office?"

Janet took a deep breath as she sat up straight, saying, "Chris, I need you to give me a pregnancy test. I haven't started menopause yet and I'm almost positive I'm pregnant, but I need to know for sure."

Amy started to cry, saying, "Janet, oh my God... You've just left Curtis and now you think you're pregnant with a fourth child? I can't even imagine what you must be feeling right now. Are you sure?"

"I'm sure. I've only been pregnant three other times in my life, and I've known every time. But it's not Curtis' child. It couldn't be. Curtis and I haven't had sex in over three months."

Amy squeezed Janet's hand. "It's okay Janet. We're here for you, no matter what. Now, whose is it?"

Janet closed her eyes and said, "Before I say, could we please verify for sure that I am pregnant?"

"Of course," Chris answered. "Let's all go to an examination room." He led Janet and Amy to the exam room down the hall.

Chris took a blood sample and said, "Okay, that's it. I'll be back in a few minutes." and he left the room.

Amy turned to Janet after Chris had left the room and said, "Janet, who's the father?"

Janet lowered her head and softly whispered into Amy's ear, "The baby is Father Richard's."

Amy took a deep cleansing breath, and said, "I knew it. I knew the two of you were having an affair. I've known you all my life, and I know you better than anyone."

Janet said, "I'm sorry I didn't confide in you sooner. It's all been so surreal and has happened so fast. One day we were friends, and the next, we were in love.

"I've never experienced anything so sensual, emotional, and spiritual, all at the same time. It's like being with him brings me closer to God. Oh, Amy, I'm powerless to the euphoria I experience when I'm with him.

"If I'm indeed pregnant, like I know I am, I feel like the pregnancy is blessed by God. It's almost like I'll be carrying the child of God inside of me. That's the only way I can describe the feelings I'm having."

"Honey, I don't know how to respond to that, except to say, if you're sure that Father Richard is who you truly want, then I'll stand beside you all the way. We are sisters till the end."

Just then, Chris came in and said, "Janet, I have the results of your test. Would you like Amy to remain in the room while I tell you?"

"Absolutely. Amy is the only person I would want with me right now.

Chris briefly paused, patted her hand, then said, "Yes Janet, you *are* pregnant."

She turned to Amy, then slowly toward Chris. She couldn't move, not even to lift a hand, as if she was paralyzed. Then she felt as if her body began to float, weightless.

Janet heard, as if it were coming from a mile away, a faint voice saying, "Janet, come back to us. Janet? Janet?"

Janet opened her eyes to find herself lying on the examination table.

"Janet, do you know where you are?" asked Chris as he shined a light in her eyes.

"What happened?" Janet asked.

"You passed out is what happened, Janet," Amy exclaimed.

Janet felt confused, saying, "For how long?"

Chris replied, "Only a minute or so. How are you feeling now?"

"I'm okay. You did say I am definitely pregnant, right Chris?"

"You are most definitely pregnant, Janet. Congratulations?"

Janet looked at Chris and then at Amy, "Congratulations indeed. I've never been happier. Thank you both so much," Janet said as she reached out to grab their hands and slowly got to her feet. "I love you both. I'll text you later, Amy."

She got into her car and sped off like she was fleeing a bank robbery.

Amy and Chris watched Janet drive away from the front door of his office, still a little dumbfounded by what had just happened. "This is going to be the biggest scandal our small city of Bridlewood has ever seen," Amy said, shaking her head, "I'm not sure who that woman is who just left, but that's not the same Janet I have known for the last forty years."

Chris said, "This is not going to end well. That's all I can say."

Janet pulled into the parking lot of the church and ran into the church to find Richard.

But no one was around. No one was at the front desk where Lily used to sit and all the offices were empty. Janet ran from office to office, but still found no one.

She walked out into the commons area and heard several women crying in the sanctuary and people talking. She ran in and found the entire church staff, as well as several parishioners, all gathered in the front pews of the church. Everyone was emotional, most of them crying.

Janet spotted Richard in the middle of the group. He was holding the hands of two different people, consoling them. Janet made her way Richard.

When he turned to her, she asked, "What's wrong? Why is everyone crying?"

Jim, the choir director, spoke up, "Janet, it's just horrible. Lily's been killed in a car accident on the outskirts of the city."

Janet put her hands to her mouth, and glanced at Richard.

Jim continued, "It happened late last night. She was with some man in a black Camry, and they apparently missed a curve and ran off an embankment. They say the car exploded into flames as it landed at the bottom of the hill. I just can't believe it. Lily is dead."

Janet sat down on the front pew beside Richard and grabbed his hand. "Oh my God. I can't believe it."

Richard bowed his head and said, "Let us pray," and he, along with everyone else, performed the sign of the cross as he began to pray, "Lord Jesus Christ, Saviour of the world, we pray for your servant Lily, and commend her to your mercy. For her sake you came down from heaven. Receive her now into the joy of your kingdom. For though she has sinned, she has not denied the Father, the Son, and the Holy Spirit, but has believed in God and has worshipped her Creator. Amen."

Everyone again made the sign of the cross, and as Janet lifted her head from prayer, she noticed Cindy walking out of the sanctuary.

As Cindy got to the door, she turned and staring directly into Janet's eyes. Then, crying softly, she made her way out of the church.

Janet followed Cindy, but all she could see was Cindy's car speeding away. Janet shook her head and closed her eyes, trying to hold back tears for Lily, tears for all of the recent events, and tears for her pregnancy. But, as hard as she tried, tears began to fall as she made her way back into the sanctuary.

When she opened the doors, the crowd was beginning to disperse. Richard remained behind with Jim. They were still praying.

Janet stood just inside the sanctuary doors, next to the baptismal font. She walked over to the font and reached in with her hand and slowly began to swirl it in the shape of an eight, over and over again.

She recalled her children being baptized in this font, and more tears rolled down her warm face. As she watched the movement of the water, she could picture each of her children being immersed in the Holy water. The water had rippled to the sides of the font as the priest raised her child back out of the water. She imagined the sensation her children must have felt as they were pulled out of the water with a spiritual cleansing.

They were only babies at the time, but she knew that God had cleansed their souls in preparation for a life devoted to God. She also knew at this moment that she'd been chosen to serve God and the Catholic Church with the child she now carried.

She thought, *This must have been the same feeling Mary had when she knew she was carrying the child of God inside her. My baby is just as blessed as Mary's Jesus, because I'm carrying the child of one of God's chosen leaders of men, his disciple.*

She felt warm all over and began to feel a spiritual cleansing seeping into her pores as she swirled her hand in the cool water, but it wasn't enough.

She felt as though God were calling her to fully immerse herself in him, in his holy water, to cleanse her soul in preparation for the child she was carrying. She knew what she had to do, to prove herself worthy of this gift that God has given her.

She grabbed the edge of the font to balance herself, and then slipped her whole body into the water. She sat down and slowly lowered her shoulders and head into the water until she was fully immersed. She held her breath for as long as she could, all the while, feeling God's love and approval flow throughout her entire body. The peace she felt was like nothing she'd ever experienced.

When she could hold her breath no longer, she rose out of the water and ran her hands from her face to the back of her head, smoothing her hair. She opened her eyes, reached for the side of the font, and stood up.

Dripping Holy water all over the sanctuary carpet, she made her way down the aisle. She kneeled before the altar, made the sign of the cross, clasped her hands together and began to silently pray.

She prayed to herself, *Lord God Almighty, I have cleansed myself in your Holy water, blessed by my true husband. I give myself to you and I give myself to Your servant, Richard. I give you this child I'm carrying, whom you've just blessed in your waters. You've given me the strength to step away from my mortal family and come into Your Holy family. I have no ties to my old family. My new life begins today. Please give Richard the strength he will need to face the scrutiny coming his way as he reveals his love for me. Please allow the Catholic Church to understand that what has happened between Richard and I is truly ordained by You. But, if they cannot, then we will follow You wherever you decide to take us. We are your servants, and we will never forsake you. Amen.*

When she finished, she remained with her head down, hands clasped together and eyes closed. She was oblivious to the crowd of church staff, school administrators, and parishioners who had returned to the sanctuary.

Father Richard stood directly behind Janet then turned to the crowd and silently gestured for everyone to leave. Then he got down on one knee beside her. He took off his jacket and put it around her, and lifted her up.

"Janet," he said, "Would you tell me what you are doing? Is it the news about Lily or is it something else? What is it, Sweetheart?"

Trembling partly from excitement and partly from a cold chill, Janet turned and looked Richard in the eyes. "Richard, I am carrying your child. I'm pregnant with a blessed child of God, a child of yours. We have been blessed by God, Himself."

She wrapped her arms around him and put her head on his shoulder. "I love you Richard. I've never known what happiness was until now. I can't wait to begin our journey together, as a family. My only true, blessed-by-God family."

Richard returned the hug in a manner which appeared consoling, since onlookers were probably looking into the sanctuary. He whispered, "I love you too, my darling. This truly is God's sign that our union is blessed. Let's go to my office and get you dried off and we'll discuss this in private. There are some people watching us right now."

"Let them watch. They're all going to know about us soon enough anyway. But I understand, and I'll abide by your wishes, my love."

They turned and left the sanctuary. Richard had his arm around her and only briefly looked up to acknowledge the crowd of people as he walked past them through the commons.

He paused at the main office and asked Jim, who was standing just inside, to please get a towel and something for Janet. They then went to his office on the second floor.

A few minutes later, Jim came in with a towel and an altar server's cassock for Janet to wear.

"This is all we could find for her." Jim said.

"This will be fine," Janet said. "I'll go home to change. Thank you, Jim."

"We all grieve for Lily in our own way, Janet. Your strength and compassion are an example for all of us to follow. God bless you, Janet," Jim said as he turned and left the office, closing the door behind him.

Richard took the towel and began to dry Janet's hair. He blotted a few strands at a time while gazing into her face.

He could see the love in her eyes. "You *are* an example for all of God's children, and I'm honored to call you my wife, and soon enough, we will stand before everyone in this church and proclaim our love. Together, we'll be an example for all the world to admire and love. We are God's chosen family, here to do his will. I know this now. We're honored to give the world the blessed child that God has placed in your womb through me, his humble servant. Great things await us, Janet, and great things await our child."

Richard knelt before Janet, held her hands and kissed them. "You are now, and henceforth will forever be, Mother Mary incarnate. I give myself to you, as you have given yourself to me and to God. Amen, I say. Amen and Hallelujah."

Richard then led her out of his office, down the stairs and into the commons outside the sanctuary. By now, there were nearly one hundred parishioners gathered. Some were in the sanctuary praying while others were consoling each other in the commons and adjoining hallway.

Father Richard, in a loud voice said, "Everyone, please join me in the sanctuary."

As everyone entered, Father Richard, holding Janet's hand, headed toward the altar. He then sat her down in his chair which was situated behind and to the left of the altar, the one he occupied during mass.

Father Richard approached the altar and said, "Would everyone please take a seat in the pews? My dear friends and children of our Lord and Savior, I would like to begin in the name of the Father, and of the Son, and of the Holy Spirit." Everyone made the sign of the cross, preparing for prayer.

Father Richard continued, "This is not just a time for grief, but also a time for celebration. Though Lily may have left this earth and all of us behind to grieve her death, she's also left to be with her Holy Father in Heaven. I'm sure she is grateful for your prayers, and your tears. But she's also rejoicing in her new home, as an honored guest of the Holy Trinity. So let's rejoice for her.

"And in the spirit of rejoicing, let's also rejoice in the miracle that God has bestowed upon us this very day. It is my humble honor, and duty, to share with you this great and holy news. Our church has been blessed with the news of a divine pregnancy. My dear Janet here—" Father Richard walked over to Janet, and led her to the altar to stand beside him.

Richard put his arm around her and continued, "—my dear Janet here has been blessed by God, through me, with a child. God has divinely blessed Janet and me with His child. We're in love with each other. She's my soulmate and gift from God, and I'm defying the Catholic Church to disallow our union as I continue to shepherd you, my dear congregation.

There were audible gasps and whispers from the large crowd.

"There is room for God and a wife in my life as a priest, and I sincerely hope you will all support us, as we struggle through the journey that lay before us. I refuse to give up without a fight, and I know that Lily would be with us, for Lily was the only person that knew about our Holy union and she was in support of it," Father Richard said, ignoring the crowd.

Everyone glanced around, confused in mind and spirit.

Father Richard held his open hands out toward his flock. "I hope and pray that you all will follow and support us, in kind. In the name of the Father, the Son and Holy Spirit, Amen." He and Janet made the sign of the cross but everyone else glanced around at one another, shocked and confused.

Richard took Janet by the hand, and without looking up or saying a word, led her out of the sanctuary, out of the church, and into his car, where he promptly kissed her.

He drove back to the rectory while Janet sat next to him in stunned silence.

Meanwhile, back at the church, the crowd of parishioners that had gathered in the sanctuary was left in dismay. They all sat in the pews, no one daring to break the lingering silence.

Then Jim's voice cut through the thick air as he spoke into the phone. "This is Jim Yancy of Our Lady of Damascus Catholic Church in Bridlewood, North Carolina. I need to speak to the Bishop, and I need to speak to him now."

15
THEY PROMISE THEM FREEDOM, BUT THEY THEMSELVES ARE SLAVES OF CORRUPTION...

Cindy headed downtown to meet Curtis. She had called him but he didn't answer. She left a voicemail, "Curtis, it's Cindy. Lily and Steamboat were killed last night in a supposed car accident, and Janet is at the church. I'm on my way to your restaurant right now. Be looking for me. Dear God, what are we going to do?"

Cindy was placing her phone in the cupholder of her car when she noticed an unread email from Lily. She picked up the phone and read the email that was sent four hours earlier:

Cindy, find Curtis as soon as you can. We need to meet, tonight. Curtis has instructions on where and when. We need to reevaluate our strategy. Everything's changed. Father Richard's brother isn't the head of the family in New York. It's Father Richard.

When Cindy arrived at the restaurant, she had completely forgotten that it was closed.

She drove two blocks more, to the hotel where Curtis was staying. She got on the elevator and pushed the button for the third floor. When the elevator arrived at the third floor and the doors opened, there stood Curtis, waiting for the elevator with his phone in his hand.

He got into the elevator, pushed the button for the lobby, and said, "I just got your message and was about to call you. We need to go meet Lily in an hour. Has she contacted you?"

"Yes, I got an email from her, but I just saw it. It was sent a few hours ago, but I don't understand. Everyone said Lily was dead, that she was killed in a car accident. Is she alive?"

"She's alive. I just spoke to her five minutes ago. But she said everyone needs to keep thinking she's dead. She didn't explain how or why, but she said not to talk to anyone but you, and to meet her at shelter number four on the backside of Sugarland Park." As the elevator doors opened to the lobby, Curtis grabbed Cindy by the hand. "We have to be there in a hurry. I'll drive."

Sugarland was a large park with three impressive playgrounds where every child in Bridlewood had played at one time or another. There were also three softball fields and three little league fields. Curtis had learned to play and love the game of baseball on those fields. It always brought back good memories for Curtis when he brought his children here to play. There were also eight soccer fields. His children played soccer on those fields eight months out of every year. The recreation department of Bridlewood kept the park beautifully manicured.

A long and scenic walking trail wound its way through the woods beside a babbling creek. A campground of sorts was situated near the back of the park. It had smaller playgrounds, camping spots for tents and hammocks, outdoor showers and bathrooms, and shelters where families and organizations would have cookouts and parties.

The campground was surrounded by the largest oak trees in the area, and during this time of year, the leaves were popping with color.

As Curtis and Cindy drove toward the campground, a peppering of multicolored leaves flew up behind the Jeep like confetti at a parade. It was a weekday, so the park was quiet. At this time, in the mid-morning, only a few joggers and maintenance crews milled about.

When Curtis pulled into the parking spots for shelter #4, no one was to be found. He and Cindy got out of the Jeep and walked under the shelter. It was chilly, and the wind was blowing slightly, which made it feel cold. Cindy tried to bundle up in her lightweight, lavender-colored sweater.

Curtis, noting her shiver, took off his jacket and put it around her shoulders. "Here, This will keep you warm."

Cindy smiled as she slipped her arms into the sleeves and crossed her arms tightly in front of her torso. "Thank you Curtis. It's really cold back here."

Just then, from out of the woods beside the shelter, came Lily in jeans, a thick jean jacket, and hiking boots. She was alone. Her cheeks and nose were red from the cold air. And she looked exhausted. "Curtis. Cindy. There's been a development which I didn't anticipate, and it's my fault for not being thorough enough in my haphazard investigation into Father Richard and his family.

"It turns out, as I've mentioned, Father Richard is the head of the family. I just heard last night about this recent discovery by the FBI. While Steamboat and I were getting ready to leave town, I got a call from one of my former FBI colleagues who was helping me gather information.

"He called to warn me that Anthony, Richard's brother, had sent some guys here to make me go away, if you understand what I mean.

"So, Steamboat and I planned out the accident. We made ourselves 'publicly available' so his men would see us, and let them follow us on a curvy road out of town. We accelerated, to suggest that we were aware of their pursuit. They sped up, too.

"We'd picked the spot ahead of time. We ran off the road and were able to jump from the vehicle as it went down the embankment. Steamboat detonated some explosives which he'd placed on the gas tank, making it look as though we were killed. There's more to it, but that's pretty much it."

"So let me get this straight," Curtis exclaimed. "Richard's family was trying to kill you, you and Steamboat faked your deaths, and now you have to live a new life, like you're in witness protection?"

"How and why is this happening?" Cindy asked.

Curtis wrapped his arm around her. "I know Cindy. It doesn't seem real."

"Oh it's real, and there's more. My colleague also informed me that Father Richard's role in the family business was that of more than just the occasional attorney role. The donations his family made to the Catholic Church in America and in Rome are what facilitated his ordination as a priest into the Catholic Church.

"So basically, he bought his way into the Church. Having him removed from the Church is going to be an impossibility. If Father Richard leaves Our Lady of Damascus, it will more than likely be of his own accord. Considering his role in his family and his monetary donations, which are in the millions, to the Catholic Church, our best bet is to leave well enough alone. At least for the time being.

"I know this isn't what you want to hear Curtis, but for now, you're going to have to sit back and let this horrible abomination play out.

"If Richard decides he really wants Janet, then, unless the Pope makes an exception, he'll have to leave the priesthood and you'll have to move on with your life."

Curtis lowered his head and said, "I'm not sure I can do that Lily. That bastard can have my wife, but if he remains a priest at Our Lady of Damascus...that is unacceptable."

Lily responded, "I understand what you're saying, but remember, this is an uphill battle that you'll likely lose. I'll help as much as I can, but please hear me. We're not only fighting Richard, we're fighting the Catholic

Church that will do anything to keep a scandal from becoming public. The Catholic Church is one of the most powerful entities on earth. Add to that the corruption of Father Richard's family business, and we're going to have an impossible battle."

Curtis looked at Lily, paused for a moment, took a deep breath and whispered, "I can't stand by while this man goes unpunished for what he's done. I can live without my wife, but I can't live without some sort of justice for his horrifying behavior. He is a priest for God's sake. How can the Catholic Church allow him to continue this immoral and sinful behavior without consequences?"

Lily hugged Curtis and whispered in his ear, "I promise, he *will* have consequences, but you need to be patient. Please be patient, Curtis. Justice will come, eventually."

Lily turned to Cindy. "This will be difficult, but unfortunately, if you want to keep your job, you're going to have to let this go as well. Trust Curtis and me to fight this on our own. I'm sorry you got involved at all, but know that I love you like a sister and I always will. I promise I will, from time to time, contact you. And hopefully, one day, I'll see you again. I have to go now. I love you both."

Lily turned and disappeared into the woods.

Curtis turned to Cindy and hugged her. He whispered, "There's nothing more for me to do for now, except try and live my life as best I can and be the best father I can be. It hurts like I've never hurt before, but it is what it is.

"You know, I've always hated that saying, 'It is what it is.' What kind of bullshit is that? But I guess I'll have to learn to love it and live by it for now."

Cindy looked into Curtis' face. "It is. But, I just know that it will be okay. I know it."

With that, they got back into the Jeep. Just as Curtis placed his hand on the gear shift, Cindy reached over and nestled her hand on his and smiled. Curtis looked into her hope-filled face and smiled back. As they drove out of the park it was almost like a ticker-tape parade with dead leaves flying up behind them.

READERS GUIDE

1. Was Janet being manipulated by Father Richard as the affair progressed, or was she a willing participant?

2. Why did the author describe, in detail, Father Richard's morning routine?

3. Is it possible that there is more to Lilly's role in this story than what the author has revealed thus far?

4. Why is Janet showing signs of nervous tension at the beginning of the affair, and does she have a "psychotic break" at the end of the book or does she really believe there is "divine inspiration" at work?

5. Does the Catholic Church and it's restraints on the clergy hold some responsibility for the affair between Father Richard and Janet or do they, alone, bear the blame?

6. What does Curtis hope to gain from confronting Janet and Father Richard in the rectory?

7. What is Cindy's role in the story, and are Cindy and Curtis developing a relationship as a result of the situation?

8. Does Father Richard think he has found his late wife "reincarnated" in Janet or is he truly in love with her?

9. Does Lilly respond to her attempted murder as a retaliation or is there a more calculated reason for her returning to Bridlewood?

10. Does Father Richard think he is "untouchable" from the consequences of his actions or has he basically succumbed to his carnal instincts?

11. Is Curtis trying to save his family or is he just trying to survive?

12. Can Father Richard remain a priest after all that has transpired?